COASTAL MIST

By G. Dennis

For Patricia!

This is a work of fiction. Names, characters, businesses, places, events and incidents are either the products of the author's imagination or used in a fictitious manner. Any resemblance to actual persons, living or dead, or actual events is purely coincidental.

© 2017 George D. Le Vasseur

Lisa walked out the employee exit exhausted; it was just before 7 after a long shift. Monday's were hard, weekenders had trashed most of the rooms that she was scheduled to clean. The 9 to 6 shift on Monday's sucked. She turned left and headed up the ally toward Bennet Ave, then followed 10th along the park. At Easton she stopped suddenly, he was standing at the corner of Easton and 11th staring at her. Lisa began to shake; her knees started to buckle as she reached for her cell phone and dialed 911. He smiled at her and waved.

"911 what's your emergency?"

The Fairview bus pulled up and he turned and entered the bus, as he climbed the bus steps he blew her a kiss and smiled that slick sick smile she hated. That smile said 'you're mine'.

"911 what's your emergency?"

"He's here."

"Who is mam?"

"The man who raped me."

"Do you need a police officer?"

"Please."

Lisa leaned against the light pole, shaking and crying until the police arrived. The officer drove her to the house on North Garden where she rented a room. As they pulled up, she saw him several blocks down the street. After she got out the officer stopped him, but the protection order stated 100 yards and as of yet he had not violated that. Lisa knew she had to run and soon, but how and to where.

That night, as she packed, Amy, remembering the time she visited her mom at work with their friends Jamie and her daughter Toni, suggested they take the ferry to

Ketchikan. Although Amy had no idea where Ketchikan was, Lisa thought that would be a good idea, close to work might be easy to just slip over to the ferry dock and leave unnoticed. A quick internet search showed the next ferry left on Friday at 6PM. Lisa did not think she had that much time. He would strike fast now that he knew where she was, and he knew that she knew.

About the same time as Lisa had started her shift that Monday morning James Truelle was docking his 86-foot coastal freighter Snowbird at the marine fuel dock. This was his first run from Ketchikan to Bellingham solo and it was much harder than he thought it would be. He needed help, a seaman, or even an inexperienced seaman apprentice would be better than having to depend on dockworkers for help. At sea and in places, where there were no dockworkers it was nearly impossible. James' first deck hand spent too much time drinking; the second got an offer on an ocean-going freighter.

James unloaded the empty fuel bladders he was hauling and filled his diesel tanks, then moved over to the overnight docking at the marina. Tomorrow at dawn he would load 18,000 lbs. of cargo at the freight terminal and be bound for Craig on Prince of Wales Island by high tide. The rest of today would be cleaning, wash the boat inside and out, flush water tanks, flush sewage tanks, even hoped to get his laundry done before turn in time.

Lisa lay awake, too worried to sleep, she had to get away and she may have only tonight to do so. He would watch day and night now if he could, since he knew she had seen him. At 4, she got up and got Amy up. They each had an overstuffed backpack, and a large strapped bag for carrying over the shoulder and a large wheeled case. They quietly slipped out of the house and into the cold, wet, night air. She looked for him as she moved slowly down the drive to the street. A taxi pulled up and they loaded their bags.

This was unexpected; Hank had to run as fast as he could to get to the car. After the evening run in with the police, he had hidden it in the alley four blocks away. He did expect her to run, but not so quickly, he had thought he had time. The 10-year stint in prison did not help him here and he was huffing and puffing when he reached the car. The taxi had at least a mile or more head start, but a taxi at this hour was easy to find especially out here in this suburb. No matter, Hank was sure he knew where she was going, the bus station. Problem was no buses would leave this early; the earliest bus out of town was 8 or so. There was an 8:10AM bus headed to Tacoma and he figured she would head back to the area where she grew up. Go back to hide with her old high school girl friends who helped her before.

Hank drove around the area looking for the yellow cab for less than 5 minutes and then headed for the bus station. He would pick her up there and make sure he knew what bus she got on. He only needed to stay 100 yards away. Once he knew what bus she was on he would head south to Tacoma for his parole officer meeting. Damn cop last evening called his parole officer and he was told to be in his office in Tacoma by 9AM. Hank parked a few blocks from the bus station on a side street then walked to a good vantage point and waited.

At 4 am James was making coffee and getting dressed, the freight terminal told him to dock on the inside pier at 5AM. There would be a fork truck operator to handle his freight from the dock, and would have the manifests and bill of lading ready to go. He had to the load and be away from the pier before 6:30. An ocean going container ship would dock and need the entire dock to unload. Ninety minutes was not a lot of time to load that much freight but he was sure he could do it.

Lisa told the taxi driver to drive to the bus station, about 5 blocks from the bus station she told him to turn around and take them to the freight terminal. During her walks from the rented room to her work at the hotel she passed the freight terminal many times and normally, when she had early shifts, she had seen small freighters docked there just before sunrise. Most of these small freighters had Alaska cities painted on their hulls under the names of the ship. Lisa hoped there would be one there this morning. She intended to beg a ride on one if she could. As the taxi pulled to the gate at the freight terminal it was almost 4:55 and Lisa looked and sighed with relief as she saw a small freighter just docking. As the taxi turned and went behind the terminal building, she saw the name; Snowbird and Ketchikan Alaska painted below the name. She said to herself; 'I have a chance I need to do whatever I have to do to get us on that freighter'. She paid the cabbie and her and Amy hauled their bags to the gate, locked. Lisa looked at the vehicle gate, locked. There was guard in the small shack by the vehicle gate and he came out as they approached.

"Hello sir, my husband's ship is just docking can you let us in please?"

"What ship is that miss?"

"The Snowbird, from Ketchikan."

"Just a moment."

He disappeared inside and checked the name of the coastal freighter docking at 5AM; it was the Snowbird out of Ketchikan. Normally family or crew met at the dock was on the docking order but this was missed, not normal but not unheard of. He went out and unlocked the gate, let them through and relocked the gate, and noted that he allowed the Truelle family (wife and daughter) into the terminal to meet the Snowbird docking at 5AM.

"Thank you so much." Lisa said as he turned toward the building, he grunted and waved her off and went back inside. Once he disappeared Lisa stopped and set down her large strapped bag and unzipped her jacket, then opened two more buttons on her blouse, paused and undid a third, then released the top clip on her bra exposing most of her breasts.

"Mom you lied to him." Amy's voice was faltering; she was scared, she had never heard her mother lie. Tears streamed down her face, at nearly 11 years-old she knew the only reason her mom would be exposing her breasts like this. She was going to offer her body to the ship's crew to save her from the man who had raped her mom, and that made her feel very bad. "Mommy please don't, let's look for another way, or take the bus."

"He's waiting at the bus station for us to come, that's how he found us here." Lisa swallowed hard, fighting the fear that gripped her, "it's the only way to keep you safe." Controlling her fears, she picked up the strapped bag, flung it on her shoulder, which opened her blouse even more, and walked briskly toward the pier. Amy followed unable to control her tears.

James had one of the large pallets in the hold, he was strapping up the second when Lisa walked up.

"Sir, sir, excuse me, can … can I talk to you, ple … please?"

James, startled by her voice, turned to see a stunningly beautiful woman in her mid to late twenties and a young preteen girl that was crying, approaching him. The woman walked right up to him, wrapped her arms around him and planted a kiss on his lips. At first, James was surprised; soon he started to kiss her. As she slowly pulled away, James could see her mostly exposed breasts, she whispered "please take us to Ketchikan, I will do anything!" James struggled to pull his eyes away from her beautiful breasts, but as he did, she looked into his eyes, "as many times as you can, please sir."

James could see the terror and desperation in her eyes and felt her trembling and wondered what kind of trouble she was running from. Then his next thought, a whole world of trouble just walked into my life, I should send them away, but something in her eyes told him to help her. Help her and this child because they are worth it. Seeing the office worker walking toward them, he stepped over and hugged the girl. "I am so glad you made it" speaking loudly. James reached out, grabbed both of the wheeled bags, and whispered, "Follow me." He led them to the freighter's starboard side, jumped down, and set the bags on the deck, then he reached out picked up the girl, who was still crying, and set her on the deck and helped the woman onto the ship. James grabbed the wheeled luggage and headed aft; he looked up and said, "Be right with you" as he passed the office worker with his manifest and bill of lading. The man nodded.

James led them through the galley into the berthing area. Setting down the bags, he looked at the women "make yourselves at home but stay inside the cabin." The women smiled and nodded. He turned to the crying girl, "you're safe now. Okay?" She nodded.

"Oh and just in case I am asked what are your names?"

"I am Lisa Sutton and this is my daughter Amy, thank you for..." Lisa trailed off realizing she offered him as much sex as he could get, so he was not really helping them "... taking us" she finished.

"I am James Truelle." He closed the galley door and went back to work.

Lisa looked at the berthing area and sighed; only four bunks, well at least it was clean and very neat. She looked into the bathroom and was surprised how clean it was, everything was shiny and smelled very fresh. In the bunkroom, the lower one on the port side was obviously his and he was using both the mattress from the top bunk and the bottom. The top bunk had plastic crates two deep held in place by netting fastened to the ceiling and to the top bunk. On the starboard side, the top mattress was on the bottom bunk with the bottom bunk mattress. Lisa sat on the bunk, put her head in her hands and wept. She got her daughter onto this freighter and Amy was safe, but she knew tonight a man would touch her for the first time since her rape and it was a man she did not know. How she was going to endure it she was not sure, but she would, she had to, she had to protect her daughter. Amy sat next to her, hugged, and wept with her. For a very long time they sat hugging and crying.

James completed loading the freight into the hold and then balanced and organized the load. He took great care to secure it tightly. He was just closing the main hatches when the flatbed truck arrived with the lumber that would go on deck. Two pallets of 2 by 10's and two pallets of plywood. Once secured to the deck he put heavy vulcanized canvas tarps over them and strapped them down. He was just finishing putting away the tie down gear when the grocery truck pulled up.

"Did you get my last minute changes?"

"Yup" The driver told him as he opened the back of the refrigerated truck, "frozen stuff first" he continued as he set the first box on the gunwale of the ship. The incoming tide had now raised the gunwale of the freighter to above the pier.

James moved the first boxes over to the deck by the freezer and then the other boxes he set on the deck by the galley door. The sky was getting lighter and James looked at his watch, 6:15. Grey cloud and misty rain, had obscured the coming daylight, he needed to get moving. The loud horn of the container ship sounded and James ran to the wheelhouse and started the engines, he would have to finish stowing the groceries after he was away from the dock. He would take her to the middle of the bay and let her drift while he finished, not the best but better than paying the extra dockage fees if he did not leave on time and clear the dock before the container ship entered.

The roar of the engine brought both Lisa and Amy to their feet; they went to the galley door and looked out. The sky was lighter but the rain was getting heavier, they saw James untie the rope at the bow and coil it on the deck, then he ran to the stern out of sight. A few moments later, the ship surged forward and to the starboard slightly, then the engine revved up and the ship moved backwards. Lisa and Amy stared as the pier slipped by. The engine revved again and the bow swung to port as the ship pivoted around, the pier disappeared. Then they moved forward, Lisa, now struck by a thought that nearly buckled her knees, 'we are totally at the mercy of this man. No one knows we are on this ship except the guard and he thinks I am married to him. Dear God I hope I have done the right thing.'

James moved the Snowbird away from the dock and around the inbound freighter, giving it plenty of room. Once in the middle of the bay he put the engines in neutral and checked her drift, very slight no wind, just rain. He returned to his chores. After storing the frozen foods, he opened the galley door and hooked it open. He found Lisa and Amy standing in the galley hugging each other crying. Lisa looked at him, "Have you changed your mind, you want to go to back shore?" he asked her calmly.

"We can't go back he'll kill me and rape her."

Startled, James stopped, not just a world of trouble, but trouble that wants to murder and rape, what have I brought into my life? He looked at the two of them hugging and crying and realized that he was doing the right thing, helping them. Then he started carrying in the boxes of refrigerated goods and the dry stores and setting them on the table and counters. "I got some ice cream and some pop cycles for your girl, and some chocolate chip cookies."

Lisa stared wide-eyed, "you did, really?"

James paused looking at her, "yea, I did, figured she would like them." Then looking at Amy, "you like fudge cycles? I got some of them as well." Amy nodded smiling at James, which eased his fears; well maybe a little trouble to help them is worth it.

"They are in the freezer outside here, the big silver box," he pointed to the freezer bolted to the outside of the galley wall.

"Can I help?" Amy pipped up and both Lisa and James looked at her.

"Sure you can, I would appreciate it." James continued, "just look around and you'll figure out where everything goes, I don't care if you want to move things." Amy smiled again and nodded. James grinned yes she is worth it.

Lisa moved to James, touched his arm, and nodded toward the door. James turned and went out, Lisa followed.

"Are the any other places to sleep?"

"Sorry Lisa no there is not, this is a working boat and it was not built for comfort or privacy, it was built to haul freight. That's the only bathroom as well." James paused and by the expression on her face, he knew what was next.

"I don't want her" Lisa looked back into the galley toward Amy, "to see or hear …"

"Forget it okay," James interrupted, "just let it go, don't worry about it. You and your girl are safe from whatever you are running from. Now that you are on board my ship, I am responsible for your safety and I will not let anything or anyone hurt you. So please just relax. Okay?"

Lisa nodded "but when we have …"

James interrupted again, "you don't have to, I will not hold to that. Okay?" He continued since he did not really need an answer. "There's a lot to do right now and we can't drift for long so I need to get busy."

James went back into the galley, Amy was busy unboxing the groceries and putting them away. "Thank you honey that's very sweet of you." Amy smiled; James smiled back thinking 'damn that girl is going steal my heart with that smile.' He turned toward Lisa; she had stood just outside the galley door after James had left trying to grasp what had just taken place. "Lisa" she looked up and came back into the galley. James continued, "There are pillows and cases, and blankets and sheets in the large cabinet under the bottom bunk. I suggest you both sleep in the same bunk that way you can use both mattresses, will be more comfortable and you will stay warmer." Lisa nodded and James continued. "There are empty crates behind my full ones you can use, make sure the netting gets fastened back up, okay?" Lisa stepped into the berthing area, looked over at James' bunk, and then nodded. "It is five to seven days to get to Ketchikan, since we have to go to Craig first and it could be more if there is bad weather, so you may want to unpack just a few things. Use the small drawers under the bunk. Stow your large bags behind the crates on the top bunk. Make sure you get everything secured and tied down. There is a wool blanket in the large drawer with the mattress cover, best to put it on the mattress first then put the mattress cover over that. The ship is steel and the water cold so it can get very cold when the engine is not running."

James paused for a moment to see if she had questions. She looked into his handsome face and his delightful, yet deep-sea grey eyes but said nothing. "Please make your selves at home, I need to get us underway and out of this bay." He turned and left, they heard him on the ladder to the wheelhouse. Moments later, the engine revved and the ship moved.

Lisa went into the galley and sat down, she was confused and not certain she really understood. Amy paused in her task noticing the look on her mother's face. "Mommy what's wrong?"

Lisa looked at her daughter; tears ran down her face "I offered him sex to take us to Ketchikan, as much as he wanted."

"I know mom, I know" Amy began to cry, "You did it to save me."

Lisa reached out, pulled her daughter to her, and hugged her, "he said I don't have to, he told me it was okay, to forget it."

Amy stepped back and looked at her mom, "really, he really said it was okay, that you really don't have to?"

"Yes honey, really."

"Why?"

"I don't know honey, I don't know and I do not understand. I guess I never realized that there were men out there that would help you just because you needed help." Lisa paused, "I don't think he is gay, do you?"

"No mom he is not gay; I am really sure of that?"

"Yea me too, I am sure he is not gay."

Amy returned to her chore, completed stowing the food while Lisa made up the bed, and unpacked a few things.

"Mom, I'm hungry can we make some breakfast. Look there is bacon, sausage, and eggs. I wonder what's in the freezer." She came back with frozen waffles.

"Put those back" Lisa told her, "maybe tomorrow. I think eggs, toast and sausage are better." Lisa realized she was hungry as well; they had very little for dinner last night and nothing since.

"Amy go upstairs and ask him if he would like breakfast, tell him I am making sausage, eggs and toast."

Amy slipped on her jacket and went up the ladder to the port side and into the wheelhouse. She stopped just inside and gasped at all of the electronics, and shiny metal. "Wow this is cool."

"Hello Amy you seem to be doing better, is your mom okay?" James smiled a large broad pleasant smile at the extremely cute girl. Amy ran to him and wrapped her arms around his waist hugging him.

"Thank you so much for helping us."

Surprised, James lightly rubbed the girls back, "your very welcome Amy, I am glad that I could help you."

"Mommy is making eggs and toast and sausage, that's okay right?" Amy looked up at him and James nodded. "She wants to know if you want some too."

"No, but thank her anyway, I already had breakfast, earlier this morning."

Amy returned to galley, after eating and cleaning up they both lay down for a rest and fell asleep.

****

Hank looked at his watch anxiously, 5:45; they should have been here by now. He looked for the bright yellow taxi that had picked them up but never saw one still he waited. When 6:15 came, he went back to his car and drove past the house; there were lights on and people moving around. He parked two blocks down near a realtor sign, took out his cell phone prop and pretended to be using it. At 7:15, two young women left in separate cars. One drove right past him, he did not look up. When they left, he walked to the house, looked into the windows, surprised by a large German Shepard dog. The dog did not bark, just sat by the window staring at him, growling. Hank looked for a way to the back of the house. He climbed the fence by the garage and went to the patio door and the dog was there looking at him again. Then he started trying to open all the windows, looking for a way in.

At the corner of the house, he heard a car pull up out front then what sounded like a police radio so he ran across the back yard and scrambled over the concrete fence. A loud voice ordered him to stop but he fled across this yard to a gate that opened. He turned left ran down the street to the first alley on the opposite side and ran into the alley. Half way down he turned left through a yard and over another fence then turned right when he got to the sidewalk. Winded he slowed to a brisk walk turning right again at the second intersection. This time he went three blocks and turned right again heading back towards his car. His walk was slow to appear as an old timer out for a morning walk despite the heavy rain that was falling and the fact he did not have an umbrella.

Hank crossed North Garden Street two blocks up from the house, he saw a city police car in the street at the house and the officer appeared to be speaking to the neighbor. Apparently, seen while climbing the fence. The cops got here fast they must have been in the area. Hank went another block and then turned right and went two blocks. He slowed as he reached North Garden but the police cruiser was gone. He got in his car and drove back to his squatter shack out to the north east of the city. He was wet, cold, tired and angry, and he was going to miss his meeting with the parole officer, so in 24 hours he would be listed as having violated his parole terms and an arrest warrant would be issued. So now he had to avoid being captured while he searched for the bitch that put him in this situation. The bitch had given him the slip for now but he would find her, he had twice so far located, lost and relocated her. He would find her.

At 3:15, that afternoon Hank parked in front of the same house with the realtor sign and played with a cell phone that had no service, no battery and no screen. Did not matter, he had no idea how to use it anyway, even if it had worked. He had seen many people stopped and parked in odd places doing exactly this same thing so he figured this looked normal.

Hank waited, 4 came and went, then 4:30 passed and the street became more active. At 4:45 more cars were going both directions, mostly he did not look at passing cars or people just at the blank, black box in his hand. Just after 5 the sounds of traffic, people moving and activity increased. Starting at 5:15, he watched the house intently, at 5:35 one of the women returned, and the other at 6:18. By 9pm he was certain that she had run. Time to find that cab driver.

Hank went to the Harris street depot and spoke to the dispatcher, "sir my daughter and granddaughter were picked up at 4AM this morning on North Garden and taken to the bus station. My granddaughter believes she left her favorite stuffed bear in the back seat, can you check with the driver to see if she left it."

The man tapped some stuff on his keyboard and read something on the screen Hank could not see then went into a back room and returned, "Sorry sir nothing was turned in from that cab on that shift."

"Can I speak to the driver please maybe he forgot to turn it in."

"We do not give out that information sir."

"Please it is a very special bear to my granddaughter, was given to her by her late grandmother."

"Sorry sir, rules are rules."

Hank turned and went outside walking towards his car. At the other side of the parking lot, was a picnic table with a group of men laughing, talking and smoking. Hank approached them "are you all cab drivers?"

"Who the fuck wants to know?" Asked a muscled Hispanic man, as he walked toward Hank.

"My granddaughter left her stuffed bear in a cab this morning at about 4AM, it is very special to her." Hank begged. "They were picked up on North Garden, anyone know who the driver was?"

"What's it worth to you?" asked one of the men sitting at the table he appeared to be from the Middle East.

"A lot if you have good accurate information"

"Like 100 bucks if I tell you who the driver was?"

"125 if you point out the driver, 150 if you get him to tell me where they really went. The actual driver gets the same amount."

The driver stood and flicked his cigarette out into the nearby street. "So if I am the driver that gets me 150, and another 150 if say where I dropped them. So show me cash."

Hank pulled out his wallet "sure let's go over here by the light so I can see better." As he walked toward the streetlight closest to his car, he removed a wad of cash, mostly ones, from his wallet then stuffed the wallet back into his kakis.

The driver followed with a laugh, and a smile on his face, thinking this guys a chump. When he got to where Hank was standing, he saw the wad of bills and held out his hand. Hank slapped the money into his hand and then grabbed his hand so tightly the driver was shocked, and Hank easily pulled the driver directly to him and put a knife under his throat.

"You got 30 seconds to tell me the truth or I'll cut your fucking throat right here."

The driver gasped and croaked out "I picked up the lady and kid at just after 4, the lady said go to the bus station, but 5 blocks away from the bus station she told me to stop and turn around and take them to the freight terminal. So that's where I dropped them, at the freight terminal."

Hank looked in his eyes and could see he was not lying, "let go of the cash."

When he did, Hank pulled the cash away and swung the knife across his chest, slicing open the driver's shirt and opening a deep cut. Startled the driver fell back with a shriek as he landed on his back. Hank ran to his car and sped away, before the driver could recover and the others realized what had happened.

"What the fuck, the goddamn fucking freight terminal, that bitch has someone helping her. That goddamn son of a bitch is going to wish he never met that bitch."

Hank knew this area was going to be swarming with cops. He already heard sirens, already had this stolen car far too long, so he pulled into a darker street by Boulevard Park and abandoned the car. He walked several blocks over to the park and found a parked car with a couple of kids making out. Jerking the door open, he pulled the boy from the car and got in. Started it and backed up hitting the boy with the door as he slammed it shut. As he dropped the tranny into drive the girl opened the passenger door and leapt onto the gravel just as he grabbed for her. "Fuck" he exclaimed as he jammed the pedal to the floor swinging the passenger door closed with a bang, "she would have been fun to play with."

He drove back towards his shack house parking the car about a mile away in an over grown field filled with junked cars. He walked along the gravel road to the shack trying to figure out how he was going to find out what ship she got on and where it was going. The freight terminal was too close to the bus station and the cabbie barn to go there.

****

The coastal freighter Snowbird was making 17 knots through the Georgia Straight at just after 1 and James needed to relieve himself. He slowed the ship to 8 knots as he made the turn towards Seymour Narrows just about 40 miles away. James locked in the autopilot and went below to the head.

The berthing area was warm and a little stuffy, as he entered he saw both Lisa and Amy sound asleep. He tried to be quiet but the flushing commode woke them. James opened both portholes in the head half way to let some fresh air in. As he passed through the bunkroom

Lisa smiled at him, and Amy's face light up in a grin so cute James nearly laughed.

"What time is it?" Lisa asked, stretching out and rolling over to face him.

"13:12"

"What does that mean?"

"1:12 in the afternoon." James stated as he walked through the galley and out.

James returned to the bridge and checked the status of the autopilot and then the radar, all normal and nothing nearby so James pushed the engine RPMs back up to 17 knots. They needed to average 15 knots to get to Craig by Friday morning. James turned on his laptop and checked his freight site. Being independent his website was the way he got hauling jobs. The site gave anyone the ability to create a login and put in the freight they had to move and the dates they wanted or needed it or when it would be available and where. Often various users would work together to get full loads to reduce their costs. It was the site and his reputation for being on time, safe and insured, that made his service different, better, and him very busy. However, runs to Bellingham or Seattle were rare and profitable as these runs were full loads and normally rushed and at top dollar, these were the larger stores and construction companies, like this run to Craig.

On the site James smiled as he confirmed a 15,000 lb. load from Ketchikan to Wrangell. The freight, hardware and construction material, all normal this time of year, would be ready for pick at the freight terminal in Ketchikan at 16:00 Saturday. Starting out good for this early in the shipping season.

Lisa rubbed the sleep from her eyes and got up, they had slept very soundly for over 4 hours after eating breakfast and cleaning up. Amy crawled out of the bunk and went into the head.

"Mom how does this thing work?"

"I don't know honey, let me look." Lisa went into the head with Amy and found it too small for both, so she looked around the corner and said, "Oh I see honey, just go and then press that button there on the back."

Amy sat and went, pressed the button and giggled as the commode flushed. Lisa followed her. After washing up a little they started up toward the wheel house. Lisa grabbed a bottle of water from the galley fridge and Amy grabbed a fudge cycle from the freezer. Then they climbed the ladder and went into the ship's bridge.

The morning mist and heavy grey cloud and rain had turned, as the morning had progressed into afternoon, to broken clouds and a mix of sun and rain showers. A warm moderate breeze blew from the southwest, making it feel like spring was really here. James was hopeful for a calm crossing.

"Where are we?" Lisa asked as she looked around at land masses on both sides, "doesn't look like the ocean."

"We are passing through the Georgia Straight, to the port, left, is Vancouver Island."

"Are we in Canada?" Amy sounded startled.

"Yes we are" James replied, "we are going to use the Johnstone Straight to get to Queen Charlotte Sound and then into the Hacata Straight, then around Point Rose and across the Dixon Entrance to Prince of Wales Island." James paused and looked at Amy, "otherwise we would have to go out into the open Pacific Ocean and get pummeled by heavy seas and rain. Safer to go this way."

"What are all those places?" Lisa asked.

"Names of waterways that we will travel through between now and Friday morning when we get to Craig."

Lisa wondered how old he was and how long he'd been running this ship. "You seem to really know your way around, how long have you worked on this ship?"

"I've owned this ship for three years now and it's not really a job, it's my life. I spend ten to eleven months a year hauling freight to small isolated island communities throughout Southeastern Alaska. The rest of the year I spend doing work and maintenance on this ship."

"You live on this boat?" Amy asked as she climbed up into the navigator chair.

"Most of the time. I have a small warehouse north of Ketchikan by a boat repair yard. The warehouse has a loft that I actually call home, well it's my permanent address. The boat yard can lift her from the water and put her on the trailer and I take her the warehouse where I can work on it when the freight hauling slows during the winter."

"You've only been operating ships for three years?" Lisa asked, somewhat startled, worried about being with such an inexperienced captain.

James heard the surprise in Lisa's voice. "Before I owned the Snowbird I spent 10 years serving in the Coast Guard, before that I grew up on my grandfather's fishing boat. Fishing with my grandpa and my dad." James paused and seemed solemn and sad to Lisa. "It was my grandpa and my dad that taught me seamanship and how to navigate and be boat skipper."

"Why didn't you keep fishing?" Lisa asked cautiously, she was curious about this man, and she liked him, she liked him a lot. Lisa thought that maybe he was just a little older than she was.

"My grandpa's boat was a fifty-three-foot salmon trawler that went down in a storm off Port Alexander when I was 17. Both my dad and grandpa were lost, how I managed to live I don't know but I made it through the night and was rescued by a Coast Guard helicopter the next morning." James paused and sighed. "Enlisted in the Coast Guard after that. Spent the next ten years serving on ships, boats and stations between Anchorage and Seattle."

"How old are you?" Amy asked in that youthful unabashed way kids have when asking questions adults want to, but don't because of politeness.

"Amy, that's not a polite question to ask someone you just met," Lisa paused and to James, "Sorry."

"I am thirty years old Amy." Then to Lisa, "nothing to be sorry about" grinning he continued, "you wanted to ask too, didn't you?"

Lisa blushed and nodded, thinking this is a man I could live with, he is different than any other man I have ever met. All of the men Lisa had met or dated wanted one thing from her, to get her into bed. Once they discovered that was not something she was interested in, they left. This man was different, she was sure it was not age as several men his age had dated her and they too were basically only interested in sleeping with her. Her curiosity was getting the best of her and she had to know, why, what was different about him. She started to ask then paused and said nothing. She looked at him with interest, at 6 foot 3 he appeared muscular and strong with an olive complexion. His hands were large and appeared calloused and rough from years of work at sea. His shoulders were broad his waist narrow, strong long legs. His features were chiseled and somewhat hard, but softened and were bright when he smiled. She found him handsome and thought she would feel safe in his arms.

James knew she was curious, maybe as curious as he was. He glanced at her, then just simply looked at her intently. She is exceptionally beautiful, he thought, 5 feet 6 inches maybe taller, a round face with almond shaped eyes that are deep brown and intense. Firm breasts round and plump very shapely, tight abs and wonderful round hips with a sexy round butt. Nicely shaped legs long and strong. Her dark brown skin looked smooth, silky and flawless. James found himself strangely attracted to her, more so than other women he had met and known. He wondered what kind of trouble she was in. Her offer of sex for an escape from Bellingham did not seem to match her personality or her attitude and now appeared as an act of pure desperation on her part. Her comment of 'he'll kill me and rape her' made him nervous about who was chasing her, and why, and did she report her problems to the police. He wanted to ask, but not yet, there would be a time to ask those questions.

Lisa blushed deeply as he looked at her and she knew he was attracted to her as she was to him. Both realized that they were actually staring at each other and then their eyes met and locked, they stared into each other's eyes. Her eye's deep brown intense, strong, yet vulnerable and lonely; his, sea grey, and somewhat wild, but warm and friendly.

"Can I steer the boat?" Amy's question brought them out of the reverie with a start. James returned his attention to their course and Lisa, blushing deeply turned toward the port to look at Vancouver Island.

"Sure you can Amy, just as soon as you learn how." James replied and he and Lisa glanced at each other for a moment and both felt that a connection was just beginning.

"Okay Amy come sit here in the helmsman chair and I will show you what you need to know to steer the boat."

Amy jumped down and climbed into the tall helmsman chair fascinated by all of the instruments.

As James explained the instruments and devices at the helmsman station to Amy, Lisa moved to the starboard side and looked at the laptop open and running. Lisa felt a warmth inside her that was unfamiliar, she had never before been so interested in a man, and the feeling of wanting him to hold her was new and somewhat scary. She looked at James again as he instructed Amy and let her handle the small wheel that steered the ship. Lisa wondered if he was married, he did not wear a ring, but that's not surprising many working men do not. She wondered if he had girlfriends, thinking he did, she felt a pang of jealousy which shocked her. "Is this computer on the internet?" Lisa asked out loud and was surprised by he own voice.

"Yes" James told her in a not a big deal monotone tone voice and then went back to teaching Amy.

"How's that possible? This is your website! Wow, this is cool how can you do this?" Lisa was reading the website James used to schedule his freight loads. "You have orders being scheduled out into June and July."

"Yes this season is starting out busy and looks like it will stay that way, going to be hard to get a deckhand hired if I'm away from port all the time." James saw that Amy had the boat steering in a fairly straight line so he left her to do that while he stepped over checked out the ships web site. "The internet is from the cellular system and as long as there is cell service that is at least at 3G then we can get internet, not the fastest internet but it does work. Well most of the time." James smiled at Lisa, "You can close that if you want."

After a while, James moved back to the helm looking at the spit of land approaching to the starboard indicating the Seymour Narrows were close. "Okay Amy we are getting into some heavy currents and it looks like traffic in the narrows you better let me handle the boat."

"Okay" Amy sighed, "Can I use the internet"

"Sure, if your mom says it's okay."

"Come here honey" Lisa helped Amy into the navigator's chair and changed the site to Amy's favorite and moved to the port side and stood next to James.

As the Snowbird moved into the narrow straights between Vancouver Island and Quadra Island they began to pick up speed so James slowed the engines. As the city of Campbell River raced past, James focused on his ship and Amy was absorbed in some internet site, Lisa drew closer to James, almost touching, James glanced her way, she smiled. Her scent was intoxicating and James wanted to hug her, but kept his focus on the ship. There glances met for a moment, both smiled but the smiles were serious. James could feel her trembling, or was it himself who trembled. They stood that way, shoulder to shoulder, both trembling and silent for a long time. The narrows approached and the current increased so James slowed the boat.

"Down bound coastal freighter Seymour Narrows this is the cruise ship Points West." The radio blared and both James and Lisa startled. Lisa sighed and stepped to the left. James picked up the radio mic.

"Points West this is Snowbird, 27 captain?"

"27"

"Snowbird this is Points West can you run the eastern edge and pass port to port?"

"Points West, this is Snowbird, sure thing captain go ahead and come through I will pass you on the port side." James turned the ship to move to the right.

"Thank you Snowbird, this is Points West clear."

"This is Snowbird whiskey, tango, alpha 7162, clear."

The large cruise ship entered the narrows just before James took the Snowbird through passing within 20 yards of the large tall ship. Amy and Lisa both stared out the windows at the ships passengers. Once through the narrows James increased his speed again. Lisa looked at the digital clock 15:47 and assumed it to be close to 4 pm.

"How far are we going today?" Lisa asked.

"About 250 miles, we need to get to the Weynton Passage before we stop and anchor. At our current pace it will be about 10PM when we get there. If we are going to make Craig by Friday and Ketchikan by Saturday, then we have to keep a 15 to 17 knot average and cover 250 miles a day." James sighed, these long hauls were great money but they were hard on him. Without a deck hand it was even harder.

"What time will we start tomorrow morning?" Amy asked, sounding a little tense, "I don't like early, mornings are for sleeping."

"A night owl" Lisa explained to James, "she always has been. I am not much of a morning person either."

"I will be awake at 5AM and we will get underway at 6AM." James stated as a matter of fact, "A morning person I am, but at 15 to 17 knots it takes 14 to 16 hours to cover the 250 miles." James paused. "Bellingham to Craig is just about 700 miles depending on the route one takes. So we need to cover 250 miles per day, and I need to make delivery at the dock in Craig before 2PM on Friday so we need to cover the 250 miles." James took a deep breath. "Also while we are in protected waters I want to go as fast as is safe and as far as is safe in case we find Queen Charlotte Sound and the Dixon Entrance being battered by high seas." They both turned and looked at him. Rough water and big waves was not something either had considered. "Have either of you been at sea before?" James asked, he knew the answer would be no, just by their looks. He was right.

"Neither of us have ever been on a boat." Lisa stumbled over the words. "How, how, rough will it be?"

"Let's hope for calm seas, but prepare for a rough ride." James saw the fear and wanted to reassure them they were safe, but also wanted them to be prepared. "If there are serious storms we will stop at Port Hardy or Bull Harbor. But we can expect two to four foot swells and if you've never been out in them you'll find that it will make you feel queasy and nauseated, otherwise known as seasickness or motion sickness." James was worried about them both being seasick during the crossing through the sound. "So there are Dramamine tablets in the first aid cabinet in the galley. You may want to take them when you get up tomorrow morning."

"The boat is safe right, were not going to sink or anything right?" Amy looked scared.

"The boat is perfectly safe and can handle some pretty heavy seas. I have had her out ten to twelve foot swells to the south east of Part Alexander several times and she handles them fine. Not something a person wants to do very often because you can get tossed around a little but it is perfectly safe." James reassured them.

They seemed to accept this and grew quiet and for a while they simply sat in the wheel house and watched the beauty of the heavily forested land on either side of them slip slowly by. James was actually appreciative of the company even in the quiet as the day grew long. After the turn at West Thurlow Island James asked Amy to take the helm so he could use the head.

"Use the what?" Amy asked.

"The bathroom, on a ship I call the bathroom a head, since that is what I learned to call it." James said as Amy took the helm. Lisa watched rather surprised as her daughter steered the ship on her own after James left. About seven minutes later James returned and sat in the navigator's chair leaving Amy to steer the ship.

"You're not going to steer?" Lisa asked quietly.

"Nope, Amy is doing just fine. I can use the break and do a little position check and make sure we are on track and on time." James used the navigation computer to pinpoint their location and speed, then pulled up the Port McNeill Marina website. Using his cell-phone he called the marina and reserved an outside dock location for 10PM to 6AM.

"We are going to dock tonight?" Lisa asked.

"Yes it will be easier to dock than to anchor without a deckhand to help." James replied, studying Lisa wondering if she could handle dock lines, maybe even the anchor. "If you could help me with dock lines it would be easier that's for sure."

"I will try, what do I need to do?"

"When we get to the dock you will need to jump off onto the dock with the bow line and put it around the docking cleat. Then as that one goes tight I will toss you the stern line and you can place it around the other docking cleat." Lisa had followed James out to landing on the starboard side of the ship and James pointed out the two lines.

"I think I can handle that, doesn't sound too hard, but jumping off a moving boat makes me nervous." Lisa looked at James, concerned, "especially after dark."

"You don't have to you know, I have done it alone before, it's just easier with help."

"I would be glad to help, but I've never done anything like this."

"I am confident you're going to do excellent!"

Lisa smiled at him as he smiled at her. The connection was growing between them.

"Mom, I'm hungry, can we make something for dinner?" Amy called out to them and they entered the wheel house.

"Oh my, it's after 5 and we missed lunch." Lisa said looking at the clock, "well I assume that 17:08 is in fact 5:08 in the afternoon." Her tone was a little sarcastic as she smiled at James.

"It is indeed" and he took the wheel from Amy.

"What would you like to eat honey?" Lisa asked Amy.

"I don't know, let's go see what we can find."

"I am not picky and a plain sandwich is fine, but if you're cooking, a hot meal would be much appreciated." James looked at Lisa with a smile.

Lisa nodded and smiled at him as she and Amy went down the ladder to the deck below and into the galley.

Darkness slowly settled on Johnstone Straight and the Snowbird plowed along making 17 knots through the deepening gloom. James watched his radar closely as twilight is the most difficult time to see. After their meal, which they shared on the bridge, Amy and Lisa had cleaned up and returned to wheelhouse. All three were quiet as they watched the sunset in wonderful orange and red glow. James was happy about that, and the weather reports had indicated a quiet night and calming winds. Tomorrow's forecast was for slight breezes from the southwest and mostly sunny skies. Unusual for early April in the north eastern reaches of the Pacific Ocean. About 9 Lisa took Amy below and got her ready for bed. Amy insisted on hugging James good night and ran up to bridge to do so. James was quite tickled by this and hugged her and kissed her forehead. Amy smiled and returned below. A little later Lisa returned to the wheel house and sat quietly watching James guide the ship through the dark. Just about 9:40 James slowed the boat as they approached the lights of Port McNeill. James went over the process again and Lisa listened intently. James slowed the boat to a crawl as they approached the breakwater and rounded it facing into the marina. He brought the nose of the ship close and Lisa jumped easily onto the dock. Reversing the port screw, the ship turned and Lisa looped the line around the cleat. James put both screws in neutral and tossed the stern line and Lisa looped it over the forward cleat. The boat came to an easy stop. James shut down all of the electronics and the engine, then turned out the bridge lights and the running lights and shut and locked both wheelhouse doors. He climbed down to the deck and met Lisa at the galley door.

"You did great for your first time handling lines." James told her as they went into the galley. "Going to relax a bit and have an ale, then shower and to bed. Would you like an ale?"

"Uh, well okay, not much of a drinker, but I do like a beer occasionally."

James poured two brown ales into shaker pint glasses and handed one to Lisa and sat on the inside bench of the galley table. Lisa slid in beside him as he made room for her.

"This is good what kind of ale is this?"

"American Brown Ale, made by yours truly in my very own little brewery in my warehouse loft apartment."

Lisa smiled, "you are an independent person for sure, and you do your own thing your own way. I like that."

James smiled, "I like you also, a lot, and I would like to know more about you. Not going to pry though, only what you're willing to talk about."

"Ask, go ahead, you took a risk helping us, maybe more than you think or know. So I am willing to answer almost any question."

"Any question?" James looked at her with a mischievous grin that Lisa immediately knew she liked.

"Almost any question." Lisa paused, then "can I ask you one first, I've been thinking about this all day and I would really like to know why?"

"Why what?"

"Why you turned down the offer I made to you for taking us?"

"You offered me as much sex as I wanted to take you to Ketchikan, and you did so out of fear and desperation. You made an offer that terrified you but you did so to save your daughter's life and your own." James paused and peered deeply into Lisa's eyes. She did not need to respond or nod, her eyes told him he hit the mark perfectly. Tears welled up in her eyes and spilled down her cheeks.

"If I hold you to that, and exploit your terror and fear then I am no better than the man you're running from. In my book that would make me worse than he is." James paused again and looked once more into Lisa's eyes. "I told you this morning that while you are on this ship, I, as master and commander of this ship, am responsible for your safety and the safety of Amy. I will let nothing or no one hurt you, including myself. If I exploit your fear then I am hurting you not helping you, and please believe me when I say I will never hurt you or Amy, ever. Nor will I let anything or anyone hurt you."

Lisa looked into James soft sea grey eyes and knew she was safe, safer than she had been in a very long time. As her tears flowed and she lay her head on her arms. James wrapped his arm around her shoulders and held her and whispered gently "you're safe now, I will take care of you, both you and Amy, so let it out." For a long time, he held her and Lisa cried away the fear and loneliness and exhaustion she had inside.

After a while Lisa's tears stopped, she looked at James then looked away, "feel like a little girl, crying like that."

"Nonsense, you had a lot of stress inside you, fear and terror from fleeing something that scares you more than offering sex to a stranger." James paused and sipped his brew. "In my eyes that shows me how courageous you are, and I know you'd give your life to protect Amy, means you're a good mother. Your strong and have good qualities and a depth of character I believe I have already come to admire."

Lisa looked at him, "thank you that means so much." Her voice cracked a little, "but stop you'll have me crying again."

After a short pause; "Who are running from and why?" James turned to her, "I need to know everything so I know what to expect and understand what I am up against."

Lisa smiled at him then took a long drink of ale. "He was my stepfather, he's Amy's father, and he raped me when I was 13."

"Not a nice person."

"No he is not. When my mother married this guy he started raping me every chance he could. Broke one of my ribs the first time I fought back, but it did not stop him. I told my mom but she did not believe me, said I never liked him so I was lying about him. When he got me pregnant mom threw me out. I stayed at my friend Terri's house, and when her mom found out I was pregnant she called the police. He denied it until Amy was born, when I was 14. The judge ordered a paternity test and proved Amy was his. He was prosecuted and got 15 years for forcible rape of a minor." She swallowed hard, then took another drink of ale. "Five months ago the department of corrections notified me he was being paroled. He only served 10 years." Lisa struggled to keep the tears at bay. "I got a protection order but the judge said 100 yards was enough because the parole board says he was sorry and rehabilitated. He found where I was working and living in Tacoma. He left a note of words cut out from magazines." She looked at James, who was sitting quietly listening, looking at her admiringly.

"I gave it to the police, but there was nothing on it that proved it was him, but I knew it was him and I think Tacoma police think it was him."

"It was a threat I take it?" James was awed by this woman.

"I will rape you while she watches then I will rape her while you watch. Then she will get the pleasure of watching me strangle you slowly." Lisa again swallowed hard.

"It was cut out of magazines and newsprint, he must have worn gloves as the police found no prints." She sighed heavily and paused. James remained silent. "I knew I had to run so I went to Terri's place on the east side of Seattle, but he found me there about two weeks later. I got a tip from a friend of Terri's husband that there was a job at a fancy hotel in Bellingham. So in the middle of the night I left and went to Bellingham." Lisa paused again, took another gulp of ale, and then just finished it. Smiled at James, "this is really good."

"Thanks"

"Yesterday as I walked home from work I saw him two blocks away smiling and waving at me. I freaked out and called the police. A cop drove me the rest of the way home. Sure enough two blocks away there he was on a street corner pretending to look at a house for sale. The cop went to talk to him but there was nothing he could do as he was over 100 yards away. He was always careful to stay that distance, and he would until he was ready and by the time the cops know he's violated the protection order, I am dead and my little girl is raped." Her anger was coming through now, James could see it and feel it. "So I decided to run and not wait even 24 hours. Amy suggested taking the Ketchikan ferry since it's only a few blocks from where I work."

"Ferry leaves on Friday evenings; you didn't want to wait?"

"I didn't think I would have time. So Amy and I packed up last night and took a cab to the freight terminal. I told the cab driver to go to Bellingham Station, but a few blocks from there I told him to turn around and go to the freight terminal."

"What made you think of the freight terminal?"

"Occasionally, when I worked an early shift that starts at 6AM, I would walk by the freight terminal and see small freighters loading. I thought if I got lucky there would be one there this morning." Lisa looked up at James, smiled "I got lucky, for once I got real lucky." She smiled a smile of joy and that lit up her face to a warm glow.

James liked that smile and that glow, "so how did you get in? The guards normally don't let people in."

"I told the guard you were my husband and that we were expected and leaving with the Snowbird. So he let us in."

"Explains the kiss." James grinned that mischievous grin again, Lisa giggled. "I liked it, a lot."

Lisa blushed, "I still can't believe I showed you my tits and offered you sex. I've not let a man touch me since I was raped." Tears ran silently down her face. Looking at James "all the men I have known in my life would have insisted I fulfill my offer."

"A person who exploits a woman is not a man, more like an animal."

"You are very different than any person I have ever met." Their eyes met and she continued, "You'll help us just because we need help, and not ask for anything."

"It's how I was raised, you help others so that when you need help yourself, there are others to help you."

"That's not the world I grew up in." Lisa sighed sadly, thinking I hope it's the world Amy can grow up in.

"So your stepfather has a name."

"Hank, well Henry Theodore Dutner."

"He is a convicted sex offender, and on the sex offender registry as a child rapist." James asked thoughtfully.

"Yes he would be."

"Okay so only the taxi driver knows you came to the terminal, and the guard knows you were there and that you got on the Snowbird?"

"Yes" Lisa was curious where he was going with this, "so."

"Well, we have to assume that Hank knows that you got into a taxi at 4AM this morning. He will know what company and maybe even which cab. So it will not take him long to find the driver and either bribe or coerce the information from him. He may already know you went to the freight terminal."

Lisa was staring at James, fear returning. James saw it, "don't worry, your safe. Even if he finds us he will have to deal with me if he comes aboard my ship."

"Now we also have to assume that he has or will look on the terminal website and see that the Snowbird was the only ship docked at 5AM this morning and that the cargo was scheduled for delivery to Craig Alaska." James was setting up a plan in his head, but Lisa was growing more terrified.

"You really think he knows where I am?" Lisa was scared, how could he know in less than 24 hours.

"I am not going to underestimate an opponent; I will assume he can think through the process just as well as I can. If he can't then I have the advantage, if he can then we will not be surprised by him." James looked at Lisa, "he already stated he wants to kill you, so I assume he will kill to get to you."

Lisa nodded, "I'm so sorry. I've put you in danger."

"You're worth it." James' short, matter of fact reply, stunned Lisa into silence for a moment.

Lisa's lower lip quivered and tears flooded her eyes, she leaned her head against his shoulder "I'm worth it, really? You really feel that way."

"Yes Lisa you are; you are very definitely worth fighting for."

Lisa leaned against him and cried a bit. She felt cared for and like she mattered to him. It was a nice feeling, calming and warm. She sat there leaning against him until she was nearly asleep. James got her up and into her bunk with Amy. She placed her hand on his cheek and mumbled "you're a wonderful man, thank you." Then sleep took her. James covered her with a blanket and then headed to the shower and his own bunk.

****

Lieutenant Charlene Groushbury was still on her first cup of coffee that Wednesday morning when her youngest and newest detective trainee brought her his report from his night on call. Her detective staff and most of the other police officers affectionately called Charlene Charlie Grouch; she was a stickler for detail and following the rules, procedures and protocols. She was the senior police officer on the Bellingham Police Department Detective squad, which had, besides herself, 4 full time detectives, one trainee and one sergeant.

Detective trainee Dale Traung had responded last night at 22:11 to an attack on a cab driver by a man with a knife. Perpetrator was a male about 50 to 55 years of age, 5 foot 10 to 6 feet tall with ebony skin. Wearing kakis and a blue denim shirt, brown loafers and no socks. He drove away in grey ford torus 4-door sedan, 2006 or a 2007. This perpetrator was seeking information from the cab drivers about a fare picked up about 4AM on North Garden Street. The fare was a young woman and a preteen girl the perpetrator stated were his daughter and granddaughter. The man wanted to know who the driver was and where they went, he offered up to $300 in cash for the information.

Saied Barth the driver cooperated and walked to the street with the man who pulled a knife and threatened him. The driver gave the man the information and the perpetrator sliced his chest open and sped off. Saied

Barth treated at St Joseph Medical Center and released. Saied Barth's written statement attached.

At 22:56, central dispatch reported a 911 caller from Boulevard Park reporting his car hijacked. John Deacon was in a parking lot in Boulevard Park just off South State Street. Mr. Deacon stated a male about 50 to 55 years old with greyish hair and ebony skin wearing kakis and a blue denim shirt that appeared to have blood on it pulled him from his car, got in, and tried to drive off with his girlfriend Jenifer Stout. The car is a dark blue 2012 Chevrolet Malibu. Both John Deacon and Jenifer Stout statements attached.

At 23:53, a patrol car found a grey torus sedan parked in an alley off 14th street four blocks from where the carjacking occurred. This car, reported stolen in Tacoma 9 days ago, is currently at the forensics unit.

Charlie agreed with Dale that these three incidents are all related and the first order of business is to identify the woman and the child from North Garden and dropped at the freight terminal.

Charlie called the cab company, got the address of the house on North Garden, and asked for the phone number that called in, but the order placed via the web site. Charlie and Dale went to the address but no one answered the door. The older man next door told them, the residents are all collage kids and either at class or work. Dale asked the man if there was a female with a preteen girl living there and he confirmed there was, but he had not seen her since she came home in police car Monday evening. He also reported that yesterday morning a male between 50 and 55 with graying hair cut short and ebony skin was looking in the windows, and had climbed the fence into the back yard so he had called police. The man was wearing kakis and a blue denim shirt, brown loafers and no socks. They thanked him and left.

On the way, back to their office, they stopped at the freight terminal and inquired what ship was here Tuesday at 5AM and did any passengers get onboard. The woman at the front desk informed them that the coastal freighter Snowbird docked at 5AM Tuesday loaded 18,000 lbs. of cargo and departed at 6:15 AM for Craig Alaska. The guard reported the wife and daughter arrived at 5AM. They boarded the Snowbird, and departed with it. The owner/operator of the Snowbird is James Truelle and the Snowbird Freight Company has a web site.

Charlene and Dale returned to their office and pulled up the patrol report logs from Monday evening. At 19:23, a Lisa Michelle Sutton had called 911 from her cell phone at the corner of Easton and 10th and reported the man who raped her was there at the corner of Easton and 11th, and he boarded the Fairview bus. The responding patrol officer drove her to her residence and noticed that the man in question two blocks away looking at a house listed for sale. The officer spoke to the man who knew there was a protection order that required him to be 100 yards from Lisa and Amy. Convicted 10 years ago for raping his stepdaughter, Mr. Dutner, released on parole five months ago, and has violated his parole and an order for his arrest issued at 9 this morning. A call to the parole officer in Tacoma informed the detectives to consider Mr. Dutner armed and dangerous and will attack and possibly murder anyone protecting Ms. Sutton and her daughter. Prior to his conviction of child rape, he was convicted of manslaughter, assault with a deadly weapon, grand theft auto, and armed robbery. Basically, Mr. Dutner was a career criminal. Charlie wondered why he was ever paroled.

Dale Traung pulled up the website for Snowbird Freight Company and easily found a phone number and dialed it. It was a cell number, and went straight to voice mail.

"This is James Truelle of Snowbird Freight Company, I am unable to take your call at this time. Please leave your name and number and the best time to contact you and I will return your call as soon as I can."

"Mr. Truelle this is Detective Dale Traung of the Bellingham Police Department please contact me at 360 537 6754 as soon as possible. Thank You."

Dale hung up the phone "must be out of service range it went straight to voice mail."

"We need to notify the Alaska State Troopers and the cities of Ketchikan and Craig. We also need to notify the TSA put a watch on the ferry terminal and call the Alaska Marine Highway people." Charlie told Dale and he wrote all of it down. "Then put out BOLO for him."

****

James' watch buzzed him awake at 5AM. He had slept soundly with very pleasant dreams of him and Lisa sailing their ship through the wonderland of southeast Alaska. He got up and made coffee and then washed up and dressed in his normal Snowbird uniform; dark blue polo with the company logo; a snowy owl in flight over a wintery tundra, the sea and mountains in the background; and heavy denim cargo pants also with the ships logo. Black leather belt with his seaman knifes and tools in pouches on the belt. White socks and high-top black canvas deck shoes finished the look, with a black ball cap with the ships logo.

James filled a large covered coffee mug, grabbed a yogurt, bagel and boiled egg from the fridge and headed to the bridge. He started the engine and then powered up the navigation equipment and all of his electronics and radar. Clicked on the marine FM radio and then the weather radio. He ate the yogurt while he listened to the weather reports for the entire area. Good weather on Queen Charlotte Sound, this morning, but warm rain moving in tonight promising dense fog throughout the area.

James untied the ship and moved it away from the dock slowly and then into the harbor. Once he rounded the point and entered the straights he took the boat to 20 knots. James wanted to make the crossing as early and as fast as possible and Sandspit was 290 miles away. He also wanted to make Craig tomorrow evening not Friday morning. He wanted to be in Ketchikan by sunset Friday, trouble was following; James' could feel it. He kept an eye on the radar, lots of fishing boats out this time of day but that radar was clear. As the first grey light of day touched the sky James noted broken clouds to the north east and clear skies to the south west.

Once the Snowbird was in open water, James locked the autopilot and turned on his computer. Cell service would be gone soon and would not return until they neared Sandspit and that would be pretty sketchy service and might not work for internet. Once online James went through the national sex offender site to link to Washington State site and looked up Henry Theodore Dutner. Sure enough he was there, James looked at the face and knew he would eventually have to deal with him. Well, maybe not, he could leave Lisa and Amy in Ketchikan to their own devices and their own fate, and that was a tempting thought, for about 15 seconds. Do as he agreed take them to Ketchikan and leave them at the dock, get his next load and go on to Wrangell with his calm peaceful life as a cargo boat skipper. Easier than tangling with a rapist hell bent on revenge. James studied the face and knew this was a man with nothing left to lose, and making Lisa pay was now his life's work. James wondered what other evil had this man perpetrated and on who, he was certain there was a lot.

James lost the internet connection and turned off the laptop, looked at his phone, still had a slight signal but that was soon gone. They had moved into the sound and two foot swells were rocking the boat so James reduced the ship's speed to 17 knots. Still fast enough to make the boat thump on the waves coming in from the port quarter.

****

Hank woke late in the morning, the shack leaked and was musty and smelled bad, but it was hidden and free and no one cared that he was there. The night's rain had filled the old rusty pots he had set out. So he washed up, rinsed his clothes and hung them up. The blood in the denim shirt did not really come out but he did not care. He put on the only other clothes he had. He started his walk to the stolen car and wondered how hot it was. Probably pretty hot so he needed to stay out of town, but needed information and the best place for that is a library, where they would have internet and computers he could use. Hank drove to nearest little gas station and parked on the side toward the rear and asked to use the phone book. Located a library in Everson, northwest about 30 minutes and headed there.

Hank found Everson to be a small community, quiet without much traffic. At the library he asked the young lad at the counter. "Do you have computers with internet I could use?"

"Sure" the lad pointed to a line of machines on tables against the back wall. "Do you have a library card?"

"No, I don't. I don't live in this area just passing through and need information on ships and freight and ferries."

"You can use the computer for an hour for $7.00 since you're not a resident." The lad handed him a card, "please complete the card and I will get you an access code."

Hank completed the card using made up information and handed it to the kid along with the $7.00. The kid looked at the card and then handed him a card with letter and number sequence.

Hank went to the computers and sat down, been a while since he had done this, and he wasn't all that good with these things. He pressed enter and the screen lit up and a little box told him that he was using a Whatcom County Library Service Computer. After a few moments the machine asked for the code and he typed it, took three tries to get it right. Then a page of text appeared and asked him to read it and agree to use it as authorized by the WCLS rules. He clicked the yes box and pressed enter. Then he was prompted to select a browser, the only symbol he recognized was the big blue lower case "e" so he clicked it. Okay this looks familiar, he typed in Bellingham and freight and right at the top of the list was the freight terminal site. He opened it and in 60 seconds had the information he needed. Snowbird from Ketchikan Alaska, but the freight was going to Craig Alaska on Prince of Wales Island. The word Craig was highlighted so he clicked it and the web page for the city of Craig opened, shit he cussed under his breath. Hard to get there and a stranger will stand out big time there. He went back to the freight site and clicked the word Snowbird. Bingo, damn freight company has a web site, what's more the damn ship's schedule is right there. "Fucking ship will be in Ketchikan on Saturday to pick up freight at the terminal in Ketchikan". I bet she will get dropped off there, bet that slut is fucking the entire crew just to get there, bitch slut. No one better touch that girl, she is mine," he realized he was actually muttering out loud. Hank was angry and starting to boil over. He took a deep breath and tried to calm himself. 'Okay, how do I get to Ketchikan?' He typed in Ketchikan and then clicked, then clicked on the city site. 'Okay can't drive so a car is worthless, plane or ferry. A plane would be dangerous, hard to hide in airports, even small ones. The ferry to Ketchikan would be a better choice.' The city site had a link and he quickly learned that the ferry leaves Friday from Bellingham at 6PM, fucking $330.00, plane ride faster but more at $450. Ok the ferry on Friday give me time to get ready; need some fake ID and cash, enough cash to buy a gun in Ketchikan. Now she will get there Saturday but I can't get there until Sunday. Well not many places to hide and nowhere to run, she'll be cornered. Only issue is if she gets off in Craig. Then I can find that out from the ship's crew, bet I can talk them into telling me where she went, like that taxi driver. One more thing, Hank did a search on picture ID cards looking for ones easy to fake or duplicate. He knew to travel he'd need one and the Washington State Department of Corrections Card he was issued when he was paroled would attract a lot of attention. He knew where to get one from a professional but that would cost, a lot. Then Hank had an idea, a dangerous one, one that could get him killed, fast, but could net him a lot dollars, fast, if he could pull it off. Once he did he would need to get out of the area and stay out. First he needed to make some changes and he could start right here at the Everson Market. Hank left the computer and walked out.

****

Lisa came into the wheel house and greeted James with a smile, "good morning."

"Good morning Lisa, you slept well?"

"I did and I slept long it seems, where are we, there is no land, are we getting into the ocean"

"We are in Queen Charlotte Sound and to the port is the Pacific Ocean and to starboard is British Columbia mainland, it's about 16 and half miles away, it's just that the coast is fogged in. Visibility is limited right now with the warm air and cold water making mist and fog."

"Are the waves going to get bigger, we are kind of going up and down and rolling?"

"I don't think it's going to get any worse than this."

"I don't feel good mommy." Amy came into the bridge and looked very pale and James knew immediately she was seasick.

"Oh honey, is your tummy upset, maybe dinner …"

James interrupted Lisa, "she is seasick or motion sickness if you like. Not much to be done about it. Drink water honey, and hang on until we get to calmer water."

Both Lisa and Amy looked at him, "your brain is not happy because the world is moving in ways your brain says it should not. It will take some time to get used to the motion and for your brain to accept a moving world." James was trying to be sympathetic. "Lisa I am surprised you're not feeling the same way."

"Who says I am not." Lisa helped Amy up it to the helmsman chair. "Just hiding it better I guess. Was feeling nauseated before I got up, it's what woke me."

"Sorry, I wish there was something I could do to help."

"Can we go where there are no waves?" Amy asked quietly.

"How long until we get out of the waves and into port or calm waters?" Lisa asked.

"From the north end of Vancouver Island to the south end of Moresby Island is about 140 miles, at 17 knots that will take us about 8 hours. So we should get to the leeward side of Moresby Island between 4 and 4:30 this afternoon."

Lisa looked at the bridge clock not quite 10AM. "I don't think I can handle six hours of this."

"In the galley first aid kit are packages of Dramamine tablets. They are 10mg, break one in half and give it to Amy and you take the other half and a whole one. They will make you drowsy but in a couple hours you will feel better." James told Lisa, "and bring up water."

Lisa returned and got Amy to swallow the pill and both sat quietly for a long time. After a while Lisa took Amy back down inside and they lay in the bunk and were soon asleep.

The day wore on and the afternoon became sunny and bright but the wind started to pick up as the day got warmer. A position check at noon told James they were making good time. By 3pm he could see the outline of Moresby Island off the port quarter and by 4 pm they were in the lee of the island and the swells started to subside so he increased the speed to 20 knots. James knew he was reducing his range going at this pace but he thought that was okay if he could get to Craig Thursday evening.

Just after 5PM Lisa and Amy woke up, both were still queasy but better and those pills had made them sleep not just drowsy. Lisa made some cool-aid for Amy and some lemon aid for her. They sat in the galley drinking it.

James came in saying hello as he passed through to the head. On the way out he asked how they were feeling.

As evening came on James increased the speed to 22 knots and got them into Queen Charlotte just before dark. Lisa had again proven good at handling lines and thinking on her feet and reacting. James was impressed, so was Amy watching her mom jump to the dock and handle those big ropes.

Once they were tied up at the marina they walked to the local pub for dinner as they all were hungry and tired, and dry, not moving, land sounded good to all of them.

James' curiosity was getting the best of him so once they were seated he asked the question foremost on his mind. "So what's in Ketchikan?" He paused, "a boyfriend?"

"No, actually was just a new place to try and hide. There is nothing there, no boyfriend, no job, no place to live." Lisa was surprised by this question. "I had to get out of Bellingham and I picked Ketchikan because it was on your boat. Snowbird Ketchikan Alaska." She paused and looked at him. His expression seemed glad or happy, perhaps amused. "So what pleases you about that?" His look of how did you know prompted Lisa to say "I can tell by your grin."

"No boyfriend pleases me a lot." James had the very mischievous grin again, Lisa liked it even more now.

"What about you, are you married, or do you have girls in every port."

"I have many acquaintances in most of the ports and some of them are females. If what you're asking if I have any female friends with benefits the answer would be mostly no, sometimes yes. I am not married, never even came close, and I am not involved in any committed relationships." looking into her eyes he continued, "at least not yet."

Lisa blushed and smiled but held his gaze, "careful you're going to scare me away."

Amy sat looking at the two adults and rolled her eyes, "why don't you two just admit you like each other and want to know each other better and be close friends."

"That's the easy part Amy, we both already know that." James paused took a deep breath like a diver about to take a deep plunge, "what's hard is to let go and fall in love, you become very vulnerable when you do." Turning to Lisa "vulnerable to being hurt and having your heart broken."

"I would not know, I am not sure I have ever been in love." Lisa swallowed hard looking into James' eyes "but I am sure your right it is very scary."

Amy looked at them as they stared into each other's eyes and giggled and mumbled something about them already being in love.

After they finished they walked back to the ship. James asked "Would you like a job?"

"Well, I do need a job, you want to hire me as your cook?" Lisa laughed thinking he was going to joke with her.

"I don't need a cook I need a deck hand." James stated seriously. "Pays $14.49 per hour, you get 12 hours pay each day we are at sea. Plus, your food and a place to live is included for the entire shipping season, for you and Amy. If you had a little experience, I would start you at 15 or 16 an hour but since I have to train you for the first month I keep it lower. After that we can increase the rate as we go. You interested?"

Lisa stopped in stunned silence for several moments, $14.49 an hour plus food and a place to live; and 12 hours pay every day. She had never earned more than minimum wage. Then she would be getting seamanship training, a valuable skill; a skill she could build on. She just looked at James for a very long moment.

"Oh, it includes health insurance, dental and vision" James added as they continued their walk.

Tears welled up in her eyes, she swallowed hard and said "Yes I am interested, very interested." She paused, did her best to get a grip on her emotions and did not really succeed "are you doing this just for me, or would you offer this to any one?"

"Well I would not normally hire a person without some training and experience, but I would have to pay a lot more. The rest would be the same, I think you have potential and skill and some guts. So for you, I am willing to train you."

Lisa moved closer to James and they looked intently at each other. "I accept. Thank you very much."

James reached out and took her hand and they stood in silence for a while. Amy stepped over and took James' other hand whispering, "I am very happy!"

They looked at each other and smiled, then continued to the ship. On board James went below deck into the cargo hold and came up with some boxes, "Lisa pick out what fits you. Since you're now a company employee you have to wear the ships uniform."

"I need to get a shower and get some rest. Tomorrows another long day." Pausing he looked at her, "your workday starts at 6AM when this ship gets underway. You have to learn how handle it in open water and maintain a straight course and how to use and read the navigation instruments."

"aye, aye captain" Lisa grinned.

All three of them slept soundly, until 5am when James' watch buzzed him awake. He washed up, dressed and made coffee. He got a yogurt, bagel and a boiled egg from the fridge and took them to the wheelhouse. He entered into a world of mist and fog. Warm air from the south had brought drizzle and fog. When he returned to the galley he heard Lisa in the head. Smiling he got a large cup of coffee and returned to the wheel house and started the engine. Just before 6AM Lisa appeared on deck, she looked wonderful in that uniform. When she looked up to the bridge and saw James nod, she jumped to the dock and released the bow line, and waited while the stern line went taught. Then when it went slack she pulled the loop off the cleat and scrambled onto the ship. Then coiled them and hung the lines. James heard his cell phone buzz. He picked it up and saw a voice mail from an unknown number. James knew from experience that cell coverage was spotty near Graham Island and in the Dixon Entrance there was none. He listened to the message. Trouble was definitely coming and he needed to get in and out of Ketchikan before 7 am Sunday.

****

Hank returned to the stolen car and noted something sticking out from under the passenger seat. He pulled out the girl's purse, dumped the contents on the seat. Some coins, and junk, and a wallet, 32 dollar's cash and more coin. A driver's license, bank card with her name Hank was sure it was reported stolen. The other card with daddy's name, William Stout, Hank wasn't sure that card would be reported stolen, but if it was he'd just make a run for it with the stuff he needed.

Hank dumped everything into the library dumpster, except the cash, coin and credit card. Then drove to the Everson Market. He pulled around to the side and parked where he figured the employee's cars were parked. He looked around for a while and after thirty minutes he got out walked over to an older pick up, a rusty faded black dodge. It was unlocked, he got in pulled out the wires and started it. Drove to the front of the store and parked close but not in view from the door, he left it running. He went in and got a backpack, two new pair of blue jeans, two new cotton button down shirts one light brown and the other forest green, He also picked out a denim jacket. He got white socks, white boxers and white cotton t-shirts. Then he found 2 hair color kits and at the pharmacy area a pair of wire rimmed reading glasses with the lowest magnification he could find. He also got deli meat, bread, cheese, mustard. Then checked out using the credit card. He tossed the card into the trash with the receipt as he went out the door. Got in the truck and headed for Tacoma.

Hank parked the truck in a brushy area behind a rusted metal warehouse that looked unused and abandoned. Crossed the lot and knocked on a small steel door. After a few moments the door opened.

"Henry Theodore, how the fuck did you get out of prison." Darrell asked slapping Hank's hands.

"Paroled about five months ago"

"Paroled how the hell you manage that."

"I found redemption in the Lord Jesus Christ, praise God almighty" Hank laughed, and continued to laugh. "Stupid bleeding hearts on parole boards, don't know shit about the real world."

Darrell laughed with him. "So, what brings you here if you're on parole you're not to be associating with guys like me?"

"Need to wash up and do a little change and get some real identification."

"Real ID's are hard to do these days, and costly." Darrell turned serious, "a good one that will fool transportation scanners are 3500, without a guarantee. Damn guaranteed one going to be 5 grand. If you got that kind of cash, I can have it for you tomorrow afternoon."

"How much you need upfront."

"None from you friend you always been good on your debt, so if you're serious then we can start."

After the picture was taken Hank asked "Darrell, is Macoco still dealing his crap from that dry docked old barge at the abandoned shipyard?"

"Macoco is dead Hank, killed in a drug war by some guys that came up from California. Mexicans I think."

"Who's dealing in his place, and where can I find him?"

"Guy named Max Fernando, has a place set up above a taco restaurant just up from the old docks." Darrell looked at Hank, "you're not dealing now are you, or using, you always hated the druggies."

"Still do hate them, just need some quick easy cash and I don't mind taking out a couple drug dealers to get it."

"Bad idea Hank, these guys are syndicated now, with lots of followers and heavy handed backers."

"Don't give a crap about syndicates, I promise I won't lead them back here."

"Good luck Hank, hope you're in the mood to do some killing because you'll have to take out more than a couple to get at Max."

Hank changed back into his older clothes and packed the new stuff into the back pack and left it with Darrell. He found the taco place, just up from the old shipping terminal and drove past it. About 2 miles away he found what he was looking for, but it took multiple trips into the five dumpsters to get all that he needed. After one more stop, he drove back behind the taco place and parked two blocks away by an apartment complex. He walked several routes to and from the taco place and then moved the truck to best location.

Hank walked back to the taco place and watched. In the back alley were two men, every hour or so they went in and different ones came out. In front just inside the door was a big guy that was supposed to be the restaurant's host, but looked like a bouncer. A lot of people went in and out but only a few stayed long enough to have actually ordered and eaten anything.

After about 11:30 things seemed to slow and by 12:30 no one was around except for the guards. Just after 1am a sporty looking two-door foreign car pulled up in back. A very nicely dressed Hispanic man got out and went in, one of the back guards followed. Hank from his position could see both front and back of the taco place and a few minutes after fancy man went in the front lights went out.

Hank started up the alley, staggering and singing to himself rather loudly. He staggered and fell and got up and pretended to be drinking from a bottle. He walked up close to the guard who had moved further into the alley when he heard him singing, then Hank swayed and fell. Hank got to his knees as the guard approached. The guard walked to Hank 'hey you, stupid drunk, get the fuck...' He never finished because Hank stuck his knife in his throat, and jumped to his feet in an attempt to avoid the volley of blood and failed. Hank dragged him to the side of building with the fire escape, dropped him to the ground, searched him and quickly found his gun. Hank looked at it, damn cheap ass nine mil. Well it will work. Hank pulled out the cut off broom handle he had hidden in his jacket and stuffed it between the rails on the fire escape just above the second step from the top. Then he went to the other side of the alley where he stashed his box of glassware. He carried the box to the side of the building opposite the fire escape. There he lit three of the wicks on the bottles. He picked up a rock, busted the kitchen window and tossed one in, it shattered against the wall just above the hot fryers and exploded, engulfing the entire kitchen. Hank tossed the second at the guy opening the back door it hit him in the face and he dove back inside screaming and covered with fire. Hank ran to the front and hit the front door with the third, breaking the glass window and exploding burning gasoline all over the host desk. The fourth and fifth were lit and thrown through the upstairs windows.

Hank ran to the fire escape and the first guy coming down had tripped and was just getting up when Hank fired a round into his head. The second guy, Mr. Fancy Man, had his hands full, carrying two large leather satchels. Hank shot him in the chest and then shot at the next guy coming out the window, that sent him back inside. Hank grabbed the bags after the fancy man fell to the bottom of the fire escape, then he turned and ran. The guy that was just exiting the window popped off several rounds, but Hank was already gone. By the time the guy from the window hit the ground Hank was driving off. He popped off more rounds, one even hit the tailgate.

Hank drove east away from the docks for at least 15 minutes, weaving through the side streets being careful to obey traffic rules. Then he drove north pretty much in straight line for 15 minutes. Then he turned east again and then south after only a mile. He followed a primary route south for 15 minutes then turned west and drove to the abandoned boatyard where Macoco used to deal and parked the truck in a brush tangle in an overgrown lot. He cut a bunch of brush and dragged junk over to conceal the truck. Then he walked to the water's edge and opened both satchels. Both had cash and what was either meth or coke. He moved the drugs into one and the cash into the other. He picked up several rocks and put them in with the drugs and then dropped in the nine mil, then tossed it in the water and watched it sink.

Hank turned his shirt inside out and then he walked the two miles to a cheap hotel and got a room. When he had counted the cash he was surprised, $15,675.00. There are going to be some real pissed off druggie's tomorrow. Hank laughed himself to sleep.

About 10AM Hank woke up and showered and dressed then turned on the TV looking for the late morning news. Sure enough local restaurant fire bombed. Three men dead and 5 others badly injured all employees no customers were hurt. Police are seeking a 40 to 50-year old man with black hair and very dark skin, anyone with information should contact Tacoma police. Hank chuckled as he walked the four miles to Darrell's abandoned warehouse.

Hank changed into his new clothes and his new look with the glasses and paid Darrell the 5 grand for the perfect looking state adult ID Card naming him as David Theodore of 1874 Darin Ave Tacoma WA. 98408. Darrell told him to give it 24 hours before using it. Takes time for the hacked updates to the state system to process through. The scan strip and mag strip on the back worked as well. He then walked to the nearest bus stop and took the bus to the Amtrak station. Then he headed north to Bellingham on the Amtrak commuter line and tomorrow evenings ferry ride to Ketchikan.

****

Dale's desk phone rang, "Detective Traung" he listened. "When, where, got a number for the store." He wrote something down and hung up. "The parent's credit card from that hijacked car was just used at the Everson Market." He told Charlene.

"Call the Everson police and have them go look for that hijacked car and tell them to get to the store to see if they have video cameras. If they do get that video."

Dale telephoned the Everson police station, when he hung up he looked at Charlene, "I don't believe this."

"Believe what?"

"Their only officer on duty is not available, and they have seen the BOLO we issued and if they see the car they will stop it and if we want the video to come get it."

"Call the store and see if they have cameras and ask them to save it for us."

Dale called the Everson Market and was told by the owner that yes he has cameras on the registers. So Dale drove to the Everson Market to get the video.

When Dale arrived at the store there was an Everson PD cruiser and a Whatcom County Sherriff car there off to the side of the building. Dale parked and walked over to the Sherriff and showed his ID. "Detective Dale Traung Bellingham PD."

"Deputy Greg Panes" they shook hands.

"That's the car hijacked from Boulevard Park." Dale stated, looking at the deputy, who nodded and motioned to the local officer to come over.

"Tom, this is Detective Traung from Bellingham PD, Detective, this is Officer Tom Shultz Everson PD." Dale and Tom shook hands. "The kid there reported his 87 dodge pickup stolen." Tom told Dale, "When I came to get the report I saw this thing and called the Sherriff's office to assist." Dale nodded.

"Well you guys can go ahead and finish up with that, I came to get video from the store. When I get it I think I can show you who stole the truck." Turning to the deputy Dale asked "you're going to have it towed to the county forensics unit in Bellingham correct?"

"That's the standard procedure and going to notify the FBI since it was hijacked, that's a reportable federal incident." Greg stated flatly to Dale.

"Tom, can I get a copy of your report when you're done, here's my card can you email it?"

"Sure thing, need copies of that video."

"Okay I will make multiples." Dale replied as he headed to the store.

Inside he was met by the manager, "you must be the Bellingham Detective?"

"Yes sir. I need to get copies of any video you may have of a male 50 to 55 years old, greying short curly hair, dark skin, wearing kakis and a blue shirt. He used a stolen credit card."

"Okay, should be easy to find." He led Dale back into the office and fifteen minutes later Dale walked out with 3 DVDs and 3 copies of the receipt showing what was purchased. He gave each of the uniformed officers a copy of the receipt and the DVD and returned to Bellingham.

Thursday morning Detective Traung is reviewing the reports from the forensics lab and preparing an activity report and an update to other agencies.

"So what is the update" Charlie asks when she got to the office at 9.

"All of the fingerprints and all of the data from the stolen Torus and the hijacked Malibu indicate that Henry Theodore Dutner was the perpetrator." Dale referred to his notes and then continued. "I am positive that he is the person that stole the 87 black dodge from Everson and we have a BOLO out for that vehicle." Dale paused for a moment looking at his supervisor. "The items purchased, new clothes, black hair dye, and glasses indicate he will be attempting to alter his appearance."

"Where is he from originally?" Charlie asks.

"Uh, Tacoma."

"Let's get with them to see if they have any reports of any incidents where a black dodge truck and our perp's description is involved. Also ask them to look for that truck. He may be seeking some falsified identification documents as well as changing his appearance, so see if they can check their sources to see if he's been around."

"Ok I will get right on that. Also had the computer guys overlay the hair dye and glasses on his prison ID picture and print up some these how he may appear now pictures." Dale added as he headed to back of the room.

Around noon Dale got an email from Tacoma PD and when he met with Charlene he covered it in detail. Apparently Tacoma PD are looking for the same person as Bellingham PD for fire-bombing a Mexican Restaurant near the docks. The restaurant was known to be a front for a Mexican drug dealer who was killed along with two of his associates. Most of the individuals in the restaurant refused to talk with police. However, citizens in the neighborhood said they saw a male 40 to 50 years old black hair and dark skin run from the scene carrying two large briefcases and drove away in an older black pickup. So the Tacoma PD has added open murder and arson charges to the list of felony warrants Henry Theodore Dutner is wanted for. Further Tacoma PD CI says Dutner was seen in the area in the afternoon and evening yesterday. Dutner is known to have associated with a known forgery expert named Darrell Cantor and was seen in the area Darrell is known to be operating in.

"So we can assume that he is heading this way with fake ID and a new a look." Charlie said. "But, how is he travelling, stolen truck is doubtful, either bus or train or a private vehicle owned by a friend or associate."

"I will get that out to all of the agencies between Tacoma and Ketchikan and make sure that the Alaska Marine Highways has this picture at their counters. We'll get him tomorrow evening when he attempts to get on that ferry." Dale strolled out back to his office.

Lisa entered the bridge "how are we going to see where we are going with all this fog?"

"Well, with radar and I think once we clear the bay it will thin out." James looked at her intently.

"What?" She smiled at him, "what, what is it?"

James grinned "you are so gorgeous. I mean you have to be the most beautiful women I have ever met. Sometimes, like right now, I want to wrap my arms around you and kiss you."

Lisa blushed, smiled and looked down. "Go ahead" she said quietly

James stepped over to her and wrapped his arms around her, Lisa looked up into his eyes, and they leaned closer slowly. Their lips met, lightly at first, then more pressure, then a glimpse of the passion they each had pent up for the last 48 hours was released. James pulled her to him tighter, she pressed into him, Lisa never felt so safe nor wanted so much to be in a man's arms. James held her firmly and tight but did not squeeze, his strong arms and hands massaged her back. The kiss went on, the boat bumped back into the dock. They parted, eyes opened and locked, a tear slipped down James' cheek and Lisa was stunned by it and by his trembling, he started to say something, she put her finger on his lips.

"Shhhhh, not yet." Lisa whispered softly.

"Okay" James replied in the same whisper. Then he released her "we need to get going, we are just drifting and that's dangerous."

James checked the radar and where the ship was in relation to the dock. Turning the wheel to port he reversed the port propeller and the ship's stern swung to port away from the dock, then he put the starboard propeller into gear and speeded it up and the ship moved forward and the swing to port increased. Lisa watched intently what he was doing, then James turned the wheel completely to starboard and pushed the port propeller to neutral, then forward and the swing to port stopped and the ship moved forward very slowly. James turned the wheel to mid-ship and watched the radar and the electronic navigation track carefully.

Slowly the Snowbird moved out of the harbor and into the bay, still moving slowly James turned the boat, following the electronic track and watching the radar. As the ship cleared the bay near Skidgate the fog lifted slightly and James increased their speed to 8 knots.

"Do you have a cell phone?" James asked quietly.

"Yes, a prepay, but I have used all of the minutes and it's turned off."

"Does Amy have a cell phone?"

"No, I could barely afford the one I have."

"Would you please go remove the battery from that phone?"

"Sure, but why?" Lisa looked a little lost.

"Just go do that and I will tell you when you get back."

When Lisa returned James explained. "The police can easily send a signal to it and turn it on and track it. They cannot however turn it off once they turn it on. So if they can track it so can Henry."

"Why would the police want to track me, and how would they even know I exist?"

James picked up his cell phone, turned it on and pressed voicemail and handed the phone to Lisa. She listened in silence and the look of worry and fear returned to her face.

"You think this message is related to Hank."

"I am positive of it. Most likely Henry used violence to get information from the cab driver, and I am sure the driver was injured in some fashion, enough to warrant a police investigation by a detective." James paused. Checked the radar and electronic navigation and with the lifting fog pushed the speed up to 12 knots. "The detective did the same thing as Henry did, looked at the terminal web site and the ships website."

"So Hank knows we are going to Craig?" Lisa was visibly shaken by this, "could he be there before us?"

"Yes he sure can if he is gutsy enough to get on airplane. Craig is a small place and I have friends there, they would already have informed me that a stranger was asking about the ship and where it was." James reached over to Lisa and put his left arm around her waist and pulled her to him, the right arm held the ships wheel. Lisa looked up at him he kissed her, "relax, I will not let him hurt you or Amy, ever. Okay?"

Lisa smiled and wrapped both arms around him, "I don't want him to hurt you." She swallowed, "you may stop him from hurting us but if you get hurt or worse doing it…" she trailed off and did not continue.

James smiled at her, "I'm a pretty tough cookie, but if he has guns then that could be a problem. I have several weapons on board but I am not what you call a good shot." He grinned a little "not terrible with a handgun, but with a long gun I can't hit the broadside of a barn."

Lisa stood there with her arms around him and his around her for a few more moments before she released him. James then adjusted the radar and increased their speed to 15 knots as the fog lifted further. "The wind is picking up" he said as he turned on the weather radio and listened for the report for the Dixon Entrance. When it came it was worrisome. "That's not good" he said. "You better go take some more Dramamine and get Amy up and give her some."

Lisa looked at him "the Dixon Entrance is where we are going?"

"We have to cross it to get to Prince of Wales Island and into Cordova Bay and that's 60 miles and at 15 knots that four hours of sea swells running four to six feet."

"Ok, I will get her up, how soon until we get there?"

"Two hours or less."

About 30 minutes later Lisa returned with Amy, who looked like she was still sleepy.

"Sorry to have to get you up but it's going to get rough, rougher than yesterday so I want you to take some Dramamine so you don't get sick."

"Is it going to be scary?"

"Well we are going to be heading pretty much directly into four to six foot waves so we are going to get bounced around a bit and up here is safer." James looked at Lisa, "did you get everything tied down and secured in the galley and bunk room?"

"Yes." She looked at James and he could see she was nervous.

An hour later as they approached Rose Point the sea swells had already picked up and the wind was now blowing briskly from the west northwest. As James made the turn at Rose Point the Snowbird encountered six-foot sea swells and building. James pushed the ship to 17 knots and told them to hang on its going to be a rough afternoon.

James was correct it was a rough and very long four hours across to Cordova Bay and he was exhausted from handing the ship and keeping her on course, but finally the heaviest seas were behind them and Cordova Bay was mostly calm and getting calmer as they went in. It was 3:30 in the afternoon and they were making good time.

"Ok it's only about 65, 70 miles to Craig, but we need to go slower here in some of the narrow places. So we should be there by 7:30 or 8 this evening."

"Mom can we get off the boat, I need to walk some." Amy was not feeling well and looked pretty worn out from being frightened and bounced about.

"I think I would like a walk as well." Lisa too was worn out and stressed.

"You will eventually get used to being on the ship and you will both learn how to move and walk even when there are waves." James paused and glanced at Lisa. "It's called getting your sea legs, and it takes a couple of days or so to get the feel of the ship and the sea."

An hour into the journey through Cordova Bay and into Tlevak Straits, Amy decided she was hungry and James figured that was a good sign. "I would like a cookie." Amy stated to the world.

"How about something not full of sugar first?" Lisa said in a most motherly voice.

"A sandwich would be great." James smiled, "if you're offering to make them?"

"Ok I can make sandwiches, come on Amy lets go."

Lisa and Amy left James on the bridge and went to the galley, and returned shortly with a sandwich and chips and dill spear for James. After eating James had Lisa take the helm so he could go below.

The trip through the straits and the narrows was uneventful and Lisa and Amy watched the land slide by. "Who lives here on all these islands?" Amy asked

"No one lives on most of these islands, they are part of the Tongass National Forest and are just wilderness." James stated. They rounded Cape Flares and James pushed the ship to 22 knots and 15 minutes later they approached Craig. James radioed the Harbor Master for an open slip and was told the freight pier was empty, he would need it to unload his cargo. As the Snowbird pulled up, Lisa jumped off to handle lines, but the mooring cleats were in odd places so she just made it up as she went. James smiled and noticed Charles and John walking toward the pier.

****

Hank arrived at Bellingham Station just after 9 and walked up Harris Ave very calmly and slowly to the business area inn where he booked a room for two nights, as David Theodore, paid cash. He slept soundly in the nice, clean and quiet room. Just after noon on Friday he went out for a walk to get the final pieces he needed.
At 3:45PM Friday David Theodore of 1874 Darin Ave Tacoma WA. 98408 walked into the Alaska Marine Highway terminal at Bellingham. David walked slowly with a shuffling gait and a cane that had a four footed end, he appeared and acted about 78 years old. His grey hair fell about his shoulders long and thick. He wore thick black rimmed glasses and heavy tweed jacket over a brown button down cotton shirt, and a clean white undershirt. He had on black dress slacks and black socks and black work shoes. Mr. Theodore had dark skin but

was dotted and speckled with flakey red and white blotches that appeared to be psoriasis.

At the check in counter David Theodore asked "is there a cabin, one way to Ketchikan available?"

"Yes sir, there are cabins available, but only four person cabins."

Mr. Theodore sighed "well, I have to get there, and I am too old to sleep on the deck."

"Yes sir, may I see your ID please."

David handed her the Washington State Adult ID card, she ran through the scanner and presto, the data on her computer was filled and the clearance was green. Mr. David Theodore of 1874 Darin Ave Tacoma WA. 98408 was 78 years old, and not on any watch or travel list.

She typed in a few items and asked "pets, bicycles, extra luggage, weapons?"

"No young lady just my back pack, got all I need." He smiled, his most pleasant smile.

"Very good sir, just a moment, ok that's $675.00" Mr. Theodore handed her cash. She walked back to a printer that printed out the tickets and returned. "Do you want to check that bag sir?"

"No thank you it's not heavy."

"Very good sir please go through the security gate to the right. Thank you and have a nice trip."

"Thank you, young lady." David replied and walked over to the security gate.

There was a TSA Officer there and a Bellingham Police Officer with printed eight and a half by eleven picture in his hand. The city cop looked at the picture and then at

David, then back at the picture. He tapped the TSA Officer and pointed out a resemblance he was seeing.

The TSA Officer asked David for his cane, and his ID and ticket. Then told him to put the back pack on the x-ray belt. He and the city officer examined the ID and the picture and then the cane, both agreed that there was a resemblance but this was not the guy and helped him through the scanner machine. On the other side, they gave him his cane and helped him with his back pack. David shuffled to the waiting area, ready to board the ship.

***------

Once they were docked and tied up the Craig Harbor Master Charles Fountain and John Kline walked over to the ship. Lisa finished up her docking chores and said "hello, I am Lisa, James' new deckhand, the girl is my daughter."

"I am Chuck, Harbor Master" he shook hands with Lisa.

"I am John, local contractor, and you're hauling my order I assume." John also shook Lisa's hand.

"I believe we are."

James came down from the bridge "Chuck good to see you been a few months. Hi John how's the building business going?"

"Since last fall James." Chuck said still looking, or perhaps ogling at Lisa. Turning to James, "we need to talk privately, as soon as possible, as in right now."

James nodded to Chuck. Then to John "If you got your trucks here I can unload right now and you can bring me the bonus check in the morning."

"I got your check right here, and damn straight I need this stuff in the morning, you're a life saver dude, getting here tonight means I can keep the crew going instead sitting around." John shook James' hand and handed him the check, "will have the trucks here in five minutes." John walked back toward the dock buildings.

"James, let's go up on the bridge, please this is urgent." Chuck urged James back to bridge.

Once there, Chuck started. "James you hired that girl or is that just a ploy to keep people from asking questions?"

"I hired her, training her to be a deck hand."

"James, the police in Bellingham Washington are looking for her." Chuck looked down at Lisa as she started with the lines on the tarps. "I don't know why they are looking for her but they also want to talk to you, they said they left you messages but you never called them back."

"Never had a chance to Chuck, and will not for a bit." James' paused, then with a very serious look on his face, "listen Chuck, the less you know the better off you are, but I know this, the police are not looking for her except to ask her questions about the criminal that raped her 10 years ago and he is hell bent on revenge."

The expression on Chuck's face was extraordinary! "You're not joking, the fucking bastard, you're protecting her?" Chuck laughed, "Poor son of bitch is going to get what he deserves." Shaking James' hand Chuck continued, "Pete's going to be here anytime, news that you docked is all over town. Hope you're expecting a party." Then as he reached the bridge door Chuck turned and asked "are you involved with her, because if you are, there's going to be some disappointed women here."

"No Chuck I am not involved with her, but I don't mind saying I have kind of fallen for her though, maybe that's not the right term but you get the idea." His grin was wide and very mischievous.

Chuck nodded went down the ladder to the main deck and told Lisa goodbye that it was great to meet her and would be seeing her in few hours. This confused Lisa so as James came down she approached him.

"Um, Chuck said he'd see us in a few hours, is he coming back?"

"Yea he'll be back, along with his wife Julie, so will John with his wife Angie. For sure Christy and Kathy will be here later, as will Pete and his wife Judy, Paul and Ann will show up as well. That's the for sure crowd, there will be others as well."

Lisa just looked at him, "what you planned a party and never told me."

"All of these people are either friends I grew up with or family friends I have known all my life. There is no plan, I dock and they show up and we talk and drink a few brews and have some steaks."

Just then John Kline and Paul his foreman showed up with flatbed trucks. Paul jumped out and ran to the Snowbird jumped on board and grabbed James and hugged him. James hugged him back. "How the heck are you doing guy? You haven't been here since last September?" Paul looked at his friend closely.

"I am doing okay, how about you and Ann? You're both coming back later?"

"We certainly are coming back later and Ann is just fine, excited to hear you docked. Glad you got in early, wasn't expecting you till tomorrow."

"Paul, this is my new deckhand and a very special friend Lisa, and that's Lisa's girl Amy over in the galley." James turned, "hey Amy come out here and meet my best friend."

Paul did not shake Lisa's hand but grabbed her and hugged her much to Lisa's surprise and he did the same to Amy when James introduced them.

"Amy, in the bottom section of the freezer is a box, can you drag it out and into the galley?" Amy nodded, James continued "put the steaks from the box into the sink, all of them." Amy smiled and headed off to do her little chore.

James moved to the boom and switched on the deck lights and tossed a life jacket then a hard hat to Lisa. "Time enough later to get caught up, we need to unload and move to my slip so I can get the grills going." James put on his jacket and hard hat and Paul headed back to his truck. Lisa looked at James with a 'you are on my list' look, a look he would learn to love and tease her about.

The unloading of the cargo went smooth and fast. Once James had taught her how the controls worked, Lisa proved very skilled at handling the crane and boom controls while James used ropes to steady and guide the loads. Once completed and John and Paul drove off, James took his hard hat and life jacket to the cabinet they are stored in and took Lisa's from her. Looking at her "your worth more than what I pay you, you're very good with those controls and that's your task from now on, and $1.00 per hour raise" he stated smiling at her.

"You're too easy" Lisa smiled and felt very proud of herself. "It's only because you like me." Lisa paused, looked at him seriously "James, the two women you named" Lisa stepped close put an arm around his neck and a hand on his chest, "Christy and Kathy", she hesitated. "Are either of them the friends with benefits you mentioned last night?" Lisa was surprised how jealous she felt.

James was very surprised and very touched by the look on Lisa's face. "Yes, both of them have been in the past." James wrapped his arms around her and pulled her close and kissed her "Lisa, I think I've fallen for you, but you know that, right?" She shook her head, "you do now." James kissed her and held her a moment.

"James, ya old smooth talker, how the hell are you?"

"Pete, good to see you. I am doing great" James moved over to gunwale and shook Pete's hand. "Come on aboard."

"You sure, because I got some official business to discuss with you and your, um, ah, friend, deckhand?"

Pete climbed aboard, "Pete this is Lisa and the girl is her daughter Amy." James paused, "I assume you want to speak to all three of us."

Pete shook hands with Amy and Lisa, "yea James I need to talk to all three of you and I have some questions for Lisa that she may want to answer in private." Pete hesitated a moment, "or maybe not after what I just saw."

"No, if it is all the same to you officer I would rather have James with me." Lisa was suddenly frightened, she thought she knew what the questioning would be about but now she was not so certain.

"Ok, Lisa that will be fine."

"Well, let me get this ship moved to the slip and then we can talk." James stated as he started up the ladder to the bridge. Amy and Pete moved over to the galley door and Lisa got the bow line off and moved aft and waited. James started the engine and moved the Snowbird forward and the aft line went slack, Lisa pulled the line off the cleat and jumped onboard. Once in the slip and tied up they went into the galley and sat around the table, Amy and Lisa crawled around onto the back bench and James and Pete on the outside.

"Okay, so let's get started." Pete looked at Lisa, "First I need to see some identification and Amy's as well."

Lisa retrieved it from the bunk room.

"Okay, so you are Lisa Sutton and this is your daughter Amy Sutton?" Pete asked while he wrote in his note book.

"Yes" Lisa looked more worried.

"Lisa do you know a Henry Theodore Dutner, and he is or was your step father?"

"Yes, he was my stepfather, my mother passed away about two years after he was convicted of raping me, ending that relationship forever." Lisa's anger was now starting to show. "He's the reason my daughter will never get to know her grandmother."

"Well that answers the next question, but I still need to know is he Amy's father, and does Amy know he is her father?"

"Yes he is my father, mom has told me the whole thing about being forced by him and how he hurt her, but mommy still loves me." Amy burst into tears and sobbed as Lisa held her and comforted her. After a bit she got up and crawled onto James' lap "my father wants to kill my mom and hurt me" she paused and snuggled into James's chest, "but James loves me and he will protect mommy and me so my father can't ever hurt me." She buried her face into James' chest and sobbed and shook.

James wrapped his arms around the child and whispered to her "yes indeed Amy I do love you and will protect you and your mommy." James looked up and saw Lisa staring at him her eyes deeply soft and a thankful. James was concerned as this was major trauma for Amy, knowing her father wants to murder her mother and hurt her.

"Well, I have the answers to those questions" Pete sighed as he looked at James holding the young girl. "I still have some hard ones to get through." He made a few more notes and then flipped the page. "Lisa, are you aware the Henry Theodore Dutner is pursuing you and that he has injured and possibly murdered people in his effort to find and capture you?"

"I am aware that he is pursuing me, I was not aware he had injured or killed anyone." Lisa looked at James, "but James figured he would threaten or injure the cab driver who dropped me and Amy at the freight terminal, in order to find out where he took me."

Pete looked at James and nodded. "Okay, do you know why he is pursuing you?"

"He has threatened to rape me and Amy and strangle me in front of Amy. He wants revenge for me telling on him when he got me pregnant when I was 13."

Pete nodded and wrote in his book. "I was asked to take you into custody by Bellingham Police Department so you could be returned to Bellingham and placed into protective custody until Dutner is apprehended."

"Pete that sounds to me like they want her for bait, to lure him in." James was upset and about to continue when Pete interrupted.

"That's what I thought and I contacted the State Troopers Office and was told that unless an arrest warrant has been issued, and Bellingham is willing to extradite then I cannot honor their request."

James relaxed a little "that's good Pete, I am not in favor of her being bait."

"Well I can however offer to escort you to the airport and notify the Alaska State Troopers that you're returning to Bellingham via Ketchikan and they would have an officer there and notify Bellingham police, so they could meet you at the airport." Pete looked at Lisa who sat motionless. "Otherwise you're free to go where you will at your own risk, knowing you're being pursued and you and Amy are in danger."

"No, I do not want an escort nor do I want protective custody, I believe that my daughter and I are safer onboard the Snowbird with James."

Pete smiled, "I happen to agree with you, but that's totally unofficial. James, you have not returned Detective Traung's calls?"

"No and I am not going to, I know what he wants and what he has to say and I have nothing to say to him. You can pass that along to him please." James told Pete flatly.

"I will pass that along to him with my report."

"Is that it Pete?" James asked as Pete put away his notebook nodding. "Good, so now let's get this party started."

"I need to go file this report and change then Judy and will I be back, make sure those steaks are rare." Pete smiled, shook hands and left.

After Pete left James got Amy to sit up "are you okay honey?" Amy nodded, James continued, "very difficult for you to think about and deal with?" Amy nodded again.

Amy scooted off his lap and stood up looking at James, "I don't understand."

James took her by the shoulders and looked into her warm and friendly brown eyes "I don't either honey, but does that matter? What matters is your mom and I love you very much and we are not going to let anything bad happen to you. Okay?"

"Promise."

"Cross my heart!" Amy hugged him. Looking at Lisa, James said "come on, we got a lot to do to get ready before my friends get here to eat steak and drink beer."

"James, how do you know these people?" Amy asked as they headed out of the galley to the main deck.

"I was born here Amy, I grew up here, I have known all of these people all my life."

"Even Christy and Kathy?" Lisa asked.

Amy recognized the tension in her voice and stopped where she was and looked at her mom. "Mom, you're jealous!"

Lisa blushed intensely then tuned around mumbling "very jealous" and went back into the galley.

Amy turned to James, eyes wide, "I've never seen my mom act like this."

Amy stood, and was again shocked to see her mom come out of the galley, walk to James and wrapped her arms around him and kissed him, passionately with lust and intensity. After several moments their lips parted. Lisa whispered "please don't go with any of the girls you've known from here, I think I would die."

James kissed her and this time it was soft and loving and tender. "I won't, promise." He held her for a while and she put her head to his chest and hugged him tightly.

The three of them quickly strung ropes and a tarp and setup tables and strung deck lights and got the grill going and soon there were 14 visitors talking and laughing and eating and drinking. The party went on into the small hours of the morning.

James, Lisa, and Amy slept late that Friday morning. James was the first to wake to make coffee and wash up and dress. He went up to the bridge and checked his web site and email. An email from the freight terminal in Ketchikan was troubling, the earliest he could dock was 6AM Sunday and the cargo was not going to be at the dock until 6:30 at the earliest. The ferry from Ketchikan would dock before they were loaded. He went to the Washington State sex offender registry and printed several copies of the picture of Henry Theodore Dutner from the site. He also grabbed the link to that registration entry and entered it in an email. The email was sent to his contacts and security people he knew at all of the docks and freight terminals in Ketchikan, Wrangell and Craig. James informed his contacts that a previous victim of this man is now employed as the deckhand on the freighter Snowbird and that the Bellingham Police Department believe he is now in pursuit of this victim and he is considered armed and dangerous. Please contact local authorities if he is seen. James also noted that he may have altered his appearance to avoid capture.

James powered off the computers and went to the galley to make a late breakfast for the Lisa, Amy and himself. Arriving he found Amy in the galley drinking juice and Lisa sitting on the bunk, her head was in her hands. James sat down next to Amy on the bench and whispered "I don't think your mommy feels very good."

Amy giggled "mommy has a hangover from drinking so much beer last night."

James got some aspirin from the first aid cabinet and a glass of water and took them to Lisa "take these, a hot shower will help some." Lisa tossed the tablets into her mouth then drank most of the water. James leaned over and kissed her on the cheek.

"I only had, oh shit did I really drink 4 beers" Lisa moaned

"Six was my count." James smiled looking at Amy.

"Yup, six is what I counted" Amy confirmed James' count.

Lisa moaned, turned a little pale then jumped up and bounced off both bunks and into the bathroom as quickly as she could and slammed the door. Retching sounds confirmed what both Amy and James' thought was about to happen.

"Mommy's not used to drinking so much, but sometimes once she starts she can't stop, at least until she passes out." Amy paused and thought a moment, "maybe that's why she doesn't drink often."

James nodded. "Well I guess its frozen waffles and juice for breakfast, at least for us. I think bacon and eggs would not be welcome, even the smell may make her very much sicker."

"Okay with me." Amy got up and went out to the freezer and got the waffles.

The shower in the bathroom started. James closed the door to the bunk room and then toasted up some frozen waffles for Amy and poured more juice. He ate his normal, yogurt and bagel and coffee. After he and Amy cleaned up James got hiking shoes and belts with canteens and a knife and a large caliber handgun and strapped it on. He had smaller ones with knives and canteens for Amy and one for Lisa.

When Lisa came out of the bunk room dressed and looking better, but still visibly sick, James gave her more aspirin and water. Then he handed her a plain bagel, she shook her head no. "You need to put something plain into your stomach or you'll get the dry heaves." Lisa nodded and took the bagel. James then strapped the belt around her waist.

"Are we going someplace?" Lisa enquired still holding the bagel and looking quite unhappy.

"You asked me to show you around Craig and the places I grew up and the house I lived in." James told her.

"You did mom, I heard you, and I told you I wanted to go see them too."

"Later" James whispered to her as he stepped closer to her "when Amy was in the galley you told me you wanted me to make love to you in those places I did with those other girls."

Lisa looked horrified, blushed, then tears welled up in her eyes. "I don't recall any of that."

"Don't worry babe, I won't hold you to that, you were really drunk, so you're forgiven, this time." James gave her that mischievous grin she loved so much.

Looking into his eyes Lisa felt the acceptance and tolerance and love he had for her and wrapped her arms around him and hugged him tightly. "Thank you, you so wonderful, I feel very lucky." She sighed deeply then looked up at him and started "I …."

James put his finger on her lips, "shhh, later." Lisa smiled and nodded.

Amy stood watching them hug with a very happy smile on her face and then joined the hug, "Can we be a family?"

"I think that is happening." James whispered cautiously.

"I think so too, and I hope it grows stronger." Lisa looked up into James eyes, never before had she desired for a man to be part of her and Amy's life.

"Come on, let's go." James smiled, "walking will help you feel better." James headed for the dock "Tramping around my old haunts will be fun." He helped them both up over the gunwale and to the dock. They walked along the dock to the parking area. From there they walked along route 924 for about a mile. James pointed out Crab Creek just ahead and then turned right on an old hiking trail that looked long unused. The trail followed the road as it curved along the shore and just above the creek it turned to the right, left the road and started to climb. The trail followed the creek for a few hundred feet and turned right again and followed a smaller creek that gurgled and bubbled away off to their left as they climbed. About 1000 feet in the trail curved and climbed steeply and soon Lisa was struggling with her headache and fell behind. James stopped at a place where he could reach the creek and there were rocks to sit on. Amy sat huffing pretty hard from the climb, Lisa came along panting heavily and sat down. James pulled off his pack and took out granola bars and gave them each one, then pulled a bandanna out of his pack and climbed down the short, steep embankment to the creek, soaked the bandanna, wrung it out and brought it back to Lisa and handed it to her. She wiped her face and neck and Amy did the same.

Lisa looked at James who did not seem to be even out of breath in the slightest, and marveled at his strength and stature and stamina and wondered when she makes love with him will he be gentle, her heart smiled inside and knew he will be extremely gentle as he is capable of such kindness. His features, though, were chiseled and hard, his arms and legs bulged out his clothes with muscle and she thought he was capable of tremendous strength and could wreak violent havoc on those whom he deemed dangerous or a threat. It was then she realized that Hank was no match for James. If Hank got close to James, James could easily break his bones and injure him severely and most likely would kill him for what he did to Lisa in the past. She sighed heavily and relaxed for the first time since she had received the letter from the Washington State Department of Corrections. She relaxed because she knew that no matter what James would protect her and Amy.

James heard the sigh and had felt her eyes on him. He turned to her "feeling better?"

"Much." Turning to Amy "ready to go on sweetheart?"

"Yes, but where are we going?"

"To the house I grew up in." James replied as he walked on up the trail.

"Your house is in the forest, I thought you grew up Craig?" Amy's face was a sight and James laughed and laughed. Lisa was still trailing along behind.

Normally this was just over a 90-minute walk for James, but with Amy and Lisa it took nearly two and half hours. The house was just about 2 miles walk from the docks but was over 2500 feet above the city overlooking a feeder creek that had no real name. The trail climbed around a bolder and came out to a small open meadow that this time of year was wet and soggy. James stopped and waited for them as they rounded the corner they both gasped. On the opposite side of the green meadow was a log cabin that still appeared regal and majestic from this distance. Behind them James pointed out Crab Bay, both Lisa and Amy gasped as they turned and took in the majestic view. Even in the grey misty light of spring, with its nearly constant drizzle, the area was beautiful and tranquil and brought peace and comfort to troubled persons caught in the hustle of modern life. James skirted the side of the meadow just inside the forest and brought them out on the opposite side of the meadow above and behind the cabin. From this point it was clear that the cabin was long ago abandoned and that local bears and other animals had been using it as shelter. The windows and doors were long ago removed by local residents who knew it was abandoned.

James walked over to a very large, long flat rock and sat down, he sighed heavily and Lisa knew he was recalling times he had lived, played and worked here in this little meadow and yard. Right in front of him was an old fire pit choked with weeds. Lisa sat on one side and Amy on the other. "There was a fire here every day, all day. My mom would cook here and bake here unless it was terrible winter snow blowing hard."

"Where is your mom now?" Lisa asked quietly.

"Not sure really, Seattle maybe. Last time I saw her she was sitting on this rock heating water to wash clothes. It was spring, just about this time of year and I was headed down to the road to walk to school. I was just about Amy's age, not yet eleven years old."

"What happened?" Amy was looking at James and could feel the sadness in him.

"She left that day, left a note to my father saying she was going back to her parent's home in Seattle. She said she was tired of being married to a man who is married to the sea and living like a pioneer was not what she wanted." Tears welled in his eyes and he brushed them away. "I learned latter from my grandpa that my dad's mom left the same way when he was about eleven as well." James gave a sad chuckle, "grandpa told me his wife said the same thing, tired of being married to a man who is married to the sea." James was silent for a time and then turned to Lisa "always been afraid of falling in love and getting married only to have my wife tell me the same thing." Tears fell down his cheeks and he hung his head. Lisa, then Amy, wrapped their arms around him and held him.

It was Amy that broke silence several minutes' latter "it is very pretty here, but there are no roads or any way to get a car or truck here." Turning to James "how did you get stuff up here, how did you get your food from the store, and there's no wires for electricity?"

James smiled at her "we carried everything up here in packs or in wheeled carts. We lived without electricity using lanterns and oil lamps." He turned and pointed to an area near the edge of the swampy, soggy area "that's where the garden was, we grew a garden and we hunted, and fished. The land gave us everything we needed to survive. I killed my first deer at age 7 just over there by that large black spruce tree." James pointed up the hill to an exceptionally large tree top standing tall above the others. They rested there for a while and then walked back to the city arriving just after 1PM and the rain began to fall very hard. So they stopped at a small bakery where they went in and got coffee and pastries, and several loafs of bread. They sat at a small table "got an email from the freight dock in Ketchikan." James sipped his coffee, "we can't dock until 6AM Sunday and the cargo will not be ready until 6:30 at the earliest." James sighed and Lisa knew this timetable was upsetting to him but she was not sure as to why.

"Does that mean we stay here or can we go to Ketchikan today?" Lisa looked at James and was curious about why he seemed so distressed about going to Ketchikan but she did not ask.

"I would like to go to Ketchikan if we can, don't you live there?" Amy looked at James and was surprised by the obvious distress he was having.

"We can go to Ketchikan today if you want, if we leave within the next hour we can get there just after the sunsets." Tears filled his eyes, looking at Lisa "please don't leave."

They both got up and hugged him. Lisa whispered "no way would I leave."

James brushed his tears away "okay we can head to Ketchikan right now. We can dock at my slip in Thomson Basin, gather up our laundry and take my truck to my loft in the warehouse. Tomorrow we can do laundry then clean and fuel the boat and get ready for cargo on Sunday morning." He smiled at them, happier than they he had been in a while "we get two nights at my place."

Lisa looked at him, she knew there was something else started to ask then stopped. Seeing her look James interjected "there are three bedrooms" smiling he turned to Amy "you get your own room."

"My own room, to keep, really?"

"Yes honey yours to keep, forever I hope." Looking at Lisa with that grin.

She put her finger to his lips "Shhh, later." James nodded.

They finished their coffee and packed up the pastries and bread and headed to the ship.

James disconnected the shore power and started taking down the lights and ropes and tarps, soon all three were soaking wet as a straight grey rain fell in a steady saturating pour. This was in fact pleasing to James, he knew straight rain like this meant no winds and calms seas. He would be able to run the ship at high speed and on the outside of Dall Island, definitely making the journey shorter and faster.

Once everything was stowed away James started the engines and Lisa handled the lines and the Snowbird slowly moved out of the slip and into the harbor. Once clear of the harbor James brought her up to 15 knots and held that speed until they passed around Suemez Island, then he increased the speed to 22 knots.

"Amy would do something for me?"

"Sure mom."

"Will you go below and get all of our clothes ready to go, put them in the laundry bags please. Sort them out so it will be easier to get the washing done. Okay?"

"Okay, mom. I guess you want to talk about adult stuff with James." Amy closed the door on the bridge as she left.

James was laughing so hard he couldn't talk for a minute. "Well she's pretty smart and very observant and a little bit of devil."

"You don't know the half of it, she can be very strong willed and independent."

"I wonder where she learned that."

Lisa smiled, "what else is bothering you about Ketchikan?" Her look was very serious and worried. "I saw it in your face at the bakery, something more than Amy and I leaving." After a short pause, "I remember that I asked to go to Ketchikan, offered you sex to take us." Lisa blushed and looked at the deck for a moment. She stepped to him and wrapped her arms around him, "you're too much of gentleman to take me up on the offer. You would rather seduce me and get me to fall for you and steal my heart, and my daughter's heart. Then you offered me a job, and I accepted and I expect to get paid, when is pay day anyway?"

"Today when we get to Ketchikan, well tonight when we get to the office in the warehouse you can fill out the paper work. I guess I can write a check but would prefer to do a direct deposit."

"I need an address, and a bank account."

"You can use my address and tomorrow morning we can stop at the bank and you can open an account. I think we could get you an Alaska ID at the county clerk."

"You're expecting me to just move right in and live with you, like we're a couple or something. So are you planning to marry me?" Lisa asked jokingly.

"Maybe I will do just that." James had that same mischievous grin and Lisa kissed his cheek.

"Okay, you side stepped the issue again. What has you worried about Ketchikan?"

"Henry Theodore Dutner."

"You think he is going to get past the police and get on that ferry tonight don't you."

"I am positive he is in Bellingham right now, not far from the ferry terminal and that he will get past the TSA and the Bellingham Police." James sighed, he knew that Henry had become his problem to deal with. Turning to Lisa "the freight terminal in Ketchikan is next to the ferry dock, we will be loading cargo as the ferry arrives Sunday morning. He will be on the deck looking for us. He will see you loading the cargo for Wrangell. He already knows we are going to Wrangell and that we have late afternoon delivery time."

Lisa snuggled closer to James, "can he get guns on the ferry?"

"Yea if he has registered firearms and permits to transport, which is unlikely. Also that would draw more unwanted scrutiny, so I think he intends to get weapons in Ketchikan, at least a handgun anyway." James paused "guns are easy to get in Alaska people sell and trade them all the time."

"So we will have time to get away from Ketchikan before he can get to us?"

"He will not attack us in Ketchikan, I know too many people. Nor in Wrangell as he will stand out there like he would in Craig. He will attack between Ketchikan and Wrangell, Sunday afternoon, if he can find us that is and if he can get a boat to take him."

"He knows how to operate a boat, he used to be a fisherman on a fishing boat in Seattle when he was young, before he stole a car and beat the owner to death with the tire jack."

James looked at Lisa "do you know if he can navigate and operate small fast boats?"

"I am sure he can he fished for years on many boats when he was kid." She paused and swallowed "he learned from his dad who had a fishing boat."

"That's good to know." James leaned over to kiss her on the cheek but she turned and their lips met kissing lightly but the feeling was closeness like partners and companions.

"You have something in mind." She paused looking at him "don't you?"

"I do and once I have thought it through we can go over it." He paused, "Henry is not so familiar with the forest or the woods is he?"

"He is not, he lived in the city or prison when he wasn't fishing."

"That could be to our advantage."

Amy returned to the bridge to find them standing next to each other her arm around his waist and his around her shoulders. "Can I steer the boat?"

"Of course you can."

Amy climbed into the helmsman's chair and took the wheel. Once she had the ship and was doing fine he went below and returned about 15 minutes later.

The remainder of the trip to Ketchikan was uneventful, the seas calm but the rain did obscure visibility some but not enough to make James worried. Just before 8 PM the Snowbird quietly and calmly docked at its normal moorings in Thomas Basin. They quickly packed up James' truck and secured the Snowbird and drove to James' warehouse just north of Peninsula Point.

"This place is cool, where's my room?" Amy was excited she had never had her own room.

James carried their suitcases down a short hall that ended at three doors. He opened the one on the left and went in setting Amy's luggage on the double bed. Amy walked around the room with her mouth open simply gasping. She opened the closet and then each drawer on the dresser and then the desk. She turned and ran to James and hugged him.

Lisa looked on thrilled to see her daughter so happy and light hearted. She placed a hand on his back and whispered in his ear "thank you so much for making her happy."

James smiled and turned and opened the center door and looked at Lisa "this one can be yours. All three rooms are about the same size and furnished the same, except mine has a king size bed, Lisa's is a queen and

Amy's is a double." Looking at the two of them as he opened the third door to the right.

It was much later than he thought it would be by the time they got everything settled and Amy to bed and Lisa entered as an employee and a check cut for her. He spent a little more time in the office finishing things, then he too headed to the shower and bed.

****

David Theodore sat quietly in the center of the waiting room with a large group of people, some sitting, some standing, some milling around. At 4:07 they announced elderly, those with young children and anyone needing help or extra time. He waited a few moments until the crowd was a little thick around the gate then rose and shuffled to the crowd of people. Twelve minutes later he was at the final check point, there was a TSA officer there and an Alaska Marine Highways security officer and a man in a suit, David figured he was a police detective.

Detective Traung was at the final check point with an eight and half by eleven picture in his hands, he would look at the picture and look at the passing passengers. When he spotted David, he looked at him intently then at the picture, then at David, then at the picture. David did not look away, or look down, he met the man's gaze and made eye contact. Traung looked again at the picture and then stepped forward as David approached.

"Sir, please step aside." Traung took David by the arm and moved him out of the line, "may I see your ID and ticket please." David handed him his ID and ticket and Traung examined them closely. "Mr. Theodore?"

"Yes" David replied hoarsely with a gravelly voice.

"What is your address sir?" Detective Traung asked.

"1874 Darin Ave Tacoma WA. 98408"

"And your phone number?"

"I do not have a phone sir" David replied softly, appearing to be embarrassed.

"Why are you going to Ketchikan?"

"To visit an old friend from the Army, we served in Vietnam together, he is a Tlingit, Haber Klopesuk, he lives in Metlakatla. His family is meeting me at Thomas Basin Sunday Morning. He's sick, man saved my life in combat."

"Thank you, sir if you would just wait here a moment." Traung stepped over to the TSA Officer and spoke to him quietly and handed him David's ID. The TSA Officer slid it through a reader on the console by the Alaska Marine Highway desk. The TSA Office spoke to Traung and handed him back the ID.

"Here you are sir thank you for being patient, have a safe trip." Traung handed David back his ID and ticket.

David nodded and walked up the Alaska Marine Highway person and got a paper indicating where his cabin was and how to get there. David followed the map to his cabin and remained there sleeping until early Saturday morning, he shuffled around the ship for an hour or so, got breakfast at the snack bar and returned to his cabin. There he planned. He would need a boat and charts of the water between Ketchikan and Wrangell, he would need a gun, preferably a 45 auto, he had Darrell make some contacts in Ketchikan to get one. He was going to pay top dollar to have it delivered to Copper Ridge library at 1:30. After the purchase he would use the library internet to locate suitable boats for sale and see if he could find an owner needing cash to meet him at the docks in the afternoon. He would take it at gunpoint if he had to and get it fueled at gunpoint. Then he would verify the freighters departure, and follow it to Wrangell, where ever that was, navigation charts would show him that. Hank figured that he would kill the crew on the ship and anchor it or run it aground. Then rape the bitch that put him in prison, then he would rape the girl. Lisa would die slowly as he strangled her and raped her again, watching her die, make the girl watch mommy die as daddy choked the life from the bitch. He fell asleep and dreamed of the event, and taking the girl to some remote island and raping her again and again.

David woke in the early evening and remained in the cabin until the night grew old and then he shuffled around the ship again and got food at the snack bar and then slept until 6AM when he packed and went up to the main deck to wait for the ship to dock.

****

James woke in small hours of the morning when Amy crawled into bed with him, she was crying. "What's the matter Amy?"

"I had a bad dream, will you hold me?"

"Sure honey."

Amy snuggled up to him and he wrapped his arms around her and held her, soon her breathing was soft and regular as sleep took her. Sleep took James shortly afterward. Just as light came to the sky James awoke again when the bed moved, this time it was Lisa. She snuggled up to him on the opposite side from Amy and he held her. Soon all three were back asleep.

Near eight James woke, both Amy and Lisa were wrapped around him, they each had their head on his chest and one arm each across his stomach. Nice but his bladder was full, he need to get up and there was no way not to wake them both.

James tried to scoot up but they woke and he got Amy to roll over so he could climb out over her and go relieve himself. He shaved, showered and 15 minutes later returned to his room with the towel around him. Both Amy and Lisa had fallen back to sleep, so he dressed in his closet and went to the kitchen to make breakfast.

The smell of bacon and potatoes woke both Lisa and then Amy. Lisa was in the shower when Amy emptied her bladder and flushed, made Lisa scream. "Sorry mommy, sorry."

"That's okay Amy, it just got hot for a moment, but say something next time."

"Breakfast smells good." Amy left the bathroom and headed to the kitchen. "Good morning James." Amy walked in and hugged him.

"Good morning honey." James hugged her tightly then said "go put some clothes on honey you can't walk around here wearing just your panties and a t-shirt."

"Why?"

"Amy, you know exactly why, go put something on!" Lisa scolded from the hall. Amy sighed and walked back to her room to get clothes.

Lisa came into the kitchen "Sorry, she has never lived in house with a man."

"That's okay, she'll figure it out. So what's up with getting in bed with me this morning. Amy came in crying said she had a bad dream, did you have a bad dream?"

"No, I had a good dream and just wanted you to hold me." Lisa brushed past him and got some coffee.

"That's good I like holding you." James glanced at her to see her smile, then returned his focus on the eggs he was scrambling.

Lisa brushed close to him again "I like you holding me, feels, comfortable." She kissed his cheek. Lisa paused for a moment like she was going to say something else, but just as she was about to James turned to her and placed his finger on her lips with "shhhhhh" sound. Lisa smiled then kissed him.

Amy returned to the kitchen dressed in jeans and work shirt and deck shoes "is this better?"

"Yes it is sweetheart." Lisa hugged her.

"That is definitely a more appropriate way for you to dress when I am around." James told her.

Amy blushed deeply, understanding more clearly why both of them were not happy with her walking around with just panties and a t-shirt. James set a plate in front of Amy and handed her a fork. Amy took the fork and began to eat. James set a plate in front of Lisa who had climbed into one of the tall stools that stood at the breakfast bar. James joined them sitting between them. They ate in silence and then quickly cleaned up and prepared to go to the boat to clean and wash and get ready to go back to sea. On the way to the boat they made several stops, bank and clothing stores and grocery all in preparation for the trip to Wrangell.

After a very long day of cleaning and loading and organizing they headed home. While Amy, then Lisa showered, James grilled the salmon a fisherman friend had given him that afternoon. Not long after eating Amy was struggling to stay awake and Lisa took her to her room and got her tucked in, James stopped in and kissed her goodnight then headed to the shower. When he finished cleaning up and left the bathroom he was surprised to see all of the lights out except his room. When he got to his room he was shocked to Lisa in his bed.

"This is surprising." James spoke quietly and softly.

"Is it really?"

"No, it's not, not really. Are you sure you're ready?"

"No, I am not sure I am ready. I know I want to, but maybe you could start just by holding me." Lisa was struggling with the conflict between her desire and her fear.

"I can do that and we can talk for a while there are things we need to discuss."

"There are things we need to say that we both have pushed to later."

"Yes those things to." Lisa looked at him questioningly.

James got in bed with her and turned out the light on the headboard. The room was dark and he snuggled up and wrapped his arms around her, they kissed passionately. They talked for some time as the moon rose, its light spilled in soft and silver through the window on to the bed. Once the bed became fully illuminated in the silver light of moon they began to kiss again and their passion intensified.

Lisa whispered "I'm ready."

****

James stood on the dock holding the guide ropes to a shrink wrapped pallet of bags of cement as Lisa lifted them and settled them into the hold. He scurried down into the hold and got the cargo boom cable lose and the guide ropes. He scrambled back to the dock and connected the next pallet, as Lisa lifted it he heard the ferry horn. The heavy coastal mist obscured it from view and by the sound it was still a little distance away. Fog was a serious issue in the narrow areas they were going to navigate today and would normally make James delay his departures, but in this case the mist was partially concealing them from the ferry. The last of the pallets were in the hold when the ferry came through, James could hear it, the size alone made it audible, and its horn was deafening. He came up on deck and looked at Lisa who was still at the controls of the cargo boom, she nodded. Both looked toward the port as the ferry approached.

David Theodore stood at the starboard rail on the main deck looking intently into the mist and fog, seeking breaks. He would occasionally get a glimpse of boats and docks and as the ferry slowed further as it approached the dock, the outline of ships became clear. The ferry slowed further and nearly came to a stop. He looked intently at the piers nearby. There a container ship appeared, it was still unloading. Then he saw it, the white over blue hull and the name showing in contrasting deep navy blue, Snowbird, Ketchikan Alaska, unique as the entire state name was painted out, not just the abbreviation. Figures on deck, looking at the ferry, yes, as if they expected him, no they were just looking at the large ferry. The fog closed in and the pier disappeared, the ferry turned and the stern of the ferry swung to port away from the freight docks as it docked on the port side at the ferry terminal. He knew where they were and he knew where they were going. He moved away from the rail and shuffled toward the port side and just forward of mid-ship where the ladder to the dock would be. There was a large crowd there already. David looked at the dock and saw police, local officers holding papers, pictures of him as he appeared when released 5 months ago. He grinned, fooled the cops before will fool them again.

As the ferry passed the Snowbird, Lisa was certain she saw him on the main deck of the ferry but there was a difference that she could not make out. She looked at James and nodded again, and he returned to the hold and completed the balancing and securing of the load. When he finished they closed the cargo hatch secured it tightly, then loaded the three pallets of lumber onto the main deck and secured them and covered them with tarps. James started the engine while Lisa stowed away the gear and checked on Amy in the cabin. Then she went to the wheelhouse. "Are we all set?"

"Yes, get the lines, he's most likely already off the ferry and may be trying to get in here."

"Are your sure the guards will stop him?"

"They will not let anyone in here without a pass, port security rules, and you only get passes from the TSA, so I doubt he would even try." James looked at her "you stay here I will get the lines." Lisa nodded.

James had to pull hard to get the stern line lose but he got it and then climbed back up to the wheel house. "We are kinda in here tight so I'll show you how we get out." Lisa stepped up close and watched.

Once in the channel James navigated by radar "get Amy up here we need another set of eyes."

"Okay." Lisa headed to the galley, returning moments later.

"What do I do?" Amy asked when she came into the wheelhouse.

"Watch behind us and to the left while your mom watches forward and right, that way I can steer using the radar and compass."

It was slow going getting out of the Tongass Narrows, James was hoping for some lifting of the mist and fog in the Clarence Straight but the unusually warm air, that moved in overnight, had covered south eastern Alaska in a damp mist. Once past Guard Island Light James picked up a little speed going from 4 knots to 6 knots.

This was worrisome as they would be easy to catch at this speed. James knew Henry would follow, he was certain he saw them as the ferry arrived and he knew where they were going. The question was would Henry figure out to follow him up the Eastern Passage and through the Narrows. Could James lure him into Earl West Cove and into the woods around the campgrounds there. Most people in Ketchikan who knew James Truelle would know he would use the Eastern Passage, he always did.

"We are going very slow how long will it take to get to Waggle?" Amy asked.

"The name of the city is Wrangell and it is on Wrangell Island and it is about a hundred and twenty miles and at this speed about 20 hours so we need to hope that as the day goes on the mist will lift and we can increase our speed." James replied with a heavy sigh. Lisa looked at him and knew he was worried.

Once into the Clarence Straights James got a better picture of the traffic around him and increased his speed to eight knots which was dangerous in this pea soup, but James needed some distance. "Keep a good watch please, I am speeding us up."

About four hours into the slow methodical trip the wind changed and started to pick up and by the time they reached Meyers Chuck the mist was lifting. When they rounded Lemesurier Point and entered Ernest Sound a brisk northwest wind was blowing cold air into south eastern Alaska. James pushed the Snowbird to 24 knots, as fast she could go, and with the wind driven chop she slapped the waves coming from the port quarter.

"Is it going to get stormy again?" Amy asked as the ship bounced a little in the chop.

"No honey it's not, in fact in about 30 minutes we'll be up by Deer Island and the wind will be blocked by Wrangell Island." James looked out through his binoculars at the narrow strip off Easton Point for any vessel traffic. Then he looked behind them for following traffic. Nothing following them yet.

****

David shuffled down the ramp to the dock, with his walker and his backpack. Moving slowly and carefully, as if his aged legs had little support. When he reached the bottom he turned and followed the others going toward the terminal, most went inside to wait for their vehicles, David side stepped the door and went around the building out toward the gate.

"Sir" a guard called after him, "you must go through the terminal to pick up your vehicle."

"I do not have one. I need a taxi to Thomas Basin." David shuffled back toward her.

"You must check out through the terminal and turn in your cabin pass."

"Oh, yeah okay, thank you."

David went into the terminal and waited in line to turn in his cabin pass. He walked past several Ketchikan police officers and nodded to them as they checked him out, but none approached him. After turning in his pass he asked the clerk where to get a taxi to take him to Thomas Basin and was told there were taxis outside in the parking lot. On the way out he picked up a tourist map of the city, found Thomas Basin, in the parking lot David found a taxi and asked for the library. On the way he saw a sign for fast food place and asked the driver to stop since he was way early. After tossing the guy a 10 he got out and headed into the fast food place and into the rest room. Hank had enough of being David and went back to Hank, thinking it would be fine now that he was here in Ketchikan. Hank was surprised to find a bulletin board with boats for sale on it with telephone numbers and contact information. There was one he was very interested in right at Thomas Basin, a 27-foot fiberglass inboard / outboard rigged for fishing. He pulled the number and then asked the kid at the counter where the nearest pay phone was. The kid looked at him like he was asked if he lived on the moon, even the manager did not know. The manager did point out that there was a phone store in this plaza. So he ordered coffee and breakfast and sat and looked at the Ketchikan map.

In the phone store he got a prepaid phone and the kid actually showed him how to use the text message. Paid in cash and used the David Theodore address, told the kid it was temporary till he got home as he dropped his over the side on the ferry, so he paid for 30 days of service. Once outside he contacted the guy with the boat and yes it was still for sale and a he could meet there today but the only time he was available was 11AM so Hank agreed.

Hank tried to call the number Darrell had given him but it just rang and rang so he tried to text and got a response, almost immediately.

Hank walked back to the fast food place, he had some time to kill so he got more coffee. A man came in about forty-five minutes later and looked around, then walked up and sat down. He had a box in his hands and he opened it so Hank could see. Sure enough a 45 semi auto with two ten round clips both full.

Hank placed an envelope on the table and the man looked at it, and then took it and got up and went out. The box was left on the seat, Hank reached out and took the box and put it in his jacket and then sat there and finished his coffee. No one seemed to even look or notice or even care. If the boat worked out he would be in pursuit of them sooner than he thought. Hank walked slowly toward Thomas Basin, he had a mile and half to walk and over two hours to do it.

Bob Gleason got to Thomas Basin about 10:45 and was greeted by Hank asking if he was the guy with the boat.

"Yea, its docked right over here." Bob led Hank out on to the docks to the third row and then out to the fifth on the right.

Hank looked at the boat walking to the bow and back. "Is there enough fuel for a test drive?"

Bob jumped into the stern of the open boat "sure, jump on board."

Hank stepped down into the boat as Bob walked toward the operators console. "What's her range with full tanks?"

"250 miles, if you go easy on her and only run her at half throttle." Bob started the engine and checked the fuel gauge. "Just a little less than a quarter tank."

Bob went forward and untied the bow, then the stern and returned to the console. "Can't go far today in this mist and fog, no radar, no sonar, no radio I took all that off for my new boat, but we can take it out and you can feel how she runs." Bob pulled the boat from slip slowly looking for traffic.

As soon as the boat cleared the dock Hank pulled out the 45 and stuck in Bob's face "now you're going to go to the fuel dock and fill this boat, then you're going to take me to Wrangell via the Eastern Passage."

Bob, quite shocked, froze for a moment "okay buddy, just relax, I ain't got no death wish I will do just what you say." Bob turned the boat to the marina fuel dock and pulled up to the pump.

Hank moved back a step and slipped the 45 under his jacket, "use a card so the guy don't have to come out."

"I have an account here I will tell him to put it on my bill." Bob waved at the kid coming down the dock, the kid waved back and then went back to the marina office.

Gary Barke did not like this, he knew the guy with Bob was a stranger and that Bob would not put fuel in a boat he was selling. Gary took note of the guy with him and made sure the cameras got his picture. Gary new Bob well, but this other guy did not belong, he had been in the marina office earlier looking at charts and asking about the Snowbird and James Truelle. That's when Gary recalled an email from James he got on Friday and went to his computer and opened his email. The picture was clear and it was the guy on Bob's boat. Gary telephoned the Ketchikan police and told them that a wanted felon from Washington State named Henry Theodore Dutner was at the marina and was possibly kidnapping Bob Gleason and stealing his boat.

Bob finished fueling the boat, he knew he needed to find a way to get off this boat. He started the boat and bumped it out away from the dock and into the harbor. As he rounded the rock wall of the harbor he gunned the engine then dove off the side and swam under water as far as he could.

Hank was caught napping, the engine surge had nearly knocked him off his feet. Hank regained his balance and had just enough time to throttle back and get control of the boat before it hit the cruise ship's mooring pier. He turned and saw the idiot in the water and was about to turn back for him when he saw the police cruiser with lights on race onto the pier. Hank throttled up the engine and disappeared into the foggy mist that still hung over the Tongass Narrows. Hank was cussing and cursing as he got the boat into the channel and headed toward Clarence Straight. He knew where the Snowbird was going and he knew the route and he knew he could catch it if the fog lifted at least a little. The 27-footer was overpowered and Hank wanted to run it at full speed, they had a four-hour head start and he wanted to catch them before Wrangell, in the narrows of the Eastern Passage would be perfect, his smaller faster boat could out maneuver the larger cargo boat.

Bob swam as hard as he could but the cold water was quickly taking its toll. Gary raced to the end of dock and tossed one of the life rings out to Bob and pulled him to the dock. Officer Tasker helped Gary haul Bob out of the water. As they headed back toward the marina office, they met BM2 Strum, a Coast Guard petty officer that was responding to the Ketchikan PD's request for assistance. In the marina office, Gary got Bob some towels and a blanket, while Bob dried off Gary told the officers what had transpired and then showed the petty office and the police officer the email from James Truelle. Bob said "that's the guy who took my boat."

"The man who sent you this email, you're talking about Chief Boatswain Mate James Truelle that owns the cargo ship Snowbird?" Petty Officer Strum asked Gary.

"Yes, that is who I am talking about, he docks it here at the basin."

"You know James?" Officer Tasker asked the petty officer.

"Yea, we served together for several years in Sitka, how do you know him?"

"Been on the Snowbird, the department uses his boat as a platform for cold water training."

"He's a great guy, real nice fella. Was here Friday night and Saturday night." Gary piped in. "The Snowbird left port this morning at 6AM heading for the freight terminal, there was women and a girl with him, new deckhand and her child I assume since the women was wearing his boats uniform. There headed to Wrangell with a load of construction material."

"Wrangell is where that guy wanted me to take him, and he specifically said through the eastern passage." Bob continued, "that's the way James will go as well, always does."

"You think he knows this guy is chasing him?" Officer Tasker asked Petty Officer Strum.

"I am very sure he does if he sent this email here to warn people about this Dutner fellow." Strum turned and headed for the door "I am going back to the station to talk to the Senior Chief, he may want to send out a patrol boat after this Dutner. Can you send that link to my email?"

"Send it to mine as well I will forward to the LT he may want to contact the State Police in Wrangell."

"Sure, on its way now." Gary clicked forward and entered the police officer and petty officers email addresses from the cards they left on the counter, then clicked send.

"Your positive he is armed you saw the gun?" Officer Tasker asked.

"45 Auto looked new except for where the serial numbers were." Bob looked at the officer. "Was gouged out bad there. He put the damn thing in my face, was hard to miss. One of those compact ones, Smith and Wesson I think, black."

"Okay thanks." Officer Tasker left.

Bob looked at Gary, "if this Dutner guy catches James in the narrows he can out maneuver him with that 27 footer."

"Yup but James knows he's following and will be expecting that, would not surprise me if James lures him in the cove there, trick him to pursue him into the woods." Gary looked at Bob then continued with a wink, "not a place I would want to have to chase James, that's his teenage playground."

✶✶

The Snowbird sailed past Eaton Point and approached Deer Island. James watched behind him closely as Lemesurier Point passed behind Brownson Island he sighed and returned his attention to sailing the Snowbird around Deer Island. Both Lisa and Amy could sense his tension and they were uneasy.

Lisa hugged him and kissed him, "you think he's following, don't you?"

"I can feel his approach; he is closer than we think but we can't see the entrance to Earnest Sound now so we will not know." He picked up his field glasses but looked forward to a thick cloud that lay over Bradfield Canal.

"Mommy I'm scared."

"I will not let anyone hurt you Amy, I promise." James set the glasses down and hugged her tightly. "So please don't worry and don't be scared. Okay?"

"Okay." Amy smiled and James' heart melted a little more.

"The running ends today honey." He looked at Lisa, "ends forever today."

Lisa wrapped her arms around him and put her head on his chest and sighed, "that's the best news I have ever heard."

Forty-five minutes later James reduced speed to 10 knots and then 8 and then 6, as they passed Point Warde. The coastal mist had settled in between high hills and cliffs of Wrangell Island and the Cleveland Peninsula of the Alaska mainland. Here the mist hung thick and wet. The cold northern wind did not reach down here to blow it away.

"This is not good, need more speed to battle the currents ahead, so we'll have to keep our eyes peeled and our senses sharp. Everyone be on your toes." James told them confidently. A few minutes later he increased the speed and turned into Blake Channel. Immediately the Snowbird slowed as they met the heavy current of the outgoing tide, James increased the engine RPMs to keep the Snowbird at the speed he wanted.

"Amy you watch forward and starboard now, Lisa you watch aft and port." As Lisa walk past he told her, "go out onto the platform and listen closely you will hear him before you see him." Lisa nodded. "When you hear the engine, tell me." James finished by kissing her and whispering, "I love you Lisa." She kissed him.

****

Just past Rock Point the mist lifted and Hank pushed the boat to maximum. Not long afterwards he rounded Guard Island Light and into Clarence Straight where the northwest wind was brisk and a solid chop forced him to slow to two third throttle. Still fast enough to catch him before he gets to Wrangell. Just over an hour later Hank rounded Lemesurier Point and swore he saw a ship just passing behind Brownson Island. The chop here was harder and the wind brisk as he turned directly into it. Hank was forced to slow even more and he cussed out loud. He had made great time and was maybe 20 miles behind but had to slow because the chop was going to tear the little boat apart if he kept it at speed. The ride from Guard Island Light to Lemesurier Point was rough on him and he was feeling it in his backside and in his arms and legs. This was going to wear him out, but he'd have her by sunset and tonight that sweet little thing would be his little tart by a warm camp fire.

Just as the Snowbird rounded Point Warde James trained his field glasses on the northwest of Deer Island and saw the small vessel approaching at high speed now.

Once Hank had gotten into the lee of the Brownson Island he had opened the little boat up and gained ground again. He could see the Snowbird just as it disappeared into the thick mist that hung in the Bradfield Canal. The mist sucked, the little boat had no radar, no sonar, no radio, but the Snowbird did and could navigate the narrow area faster with the radar than Hank could.

Five miles into the Blake Channel Lisa stepped into the wheelhouse and whispered to James "I hear an engine, it seems close but I think it's far and going slow."

James increased his speed to 10 knots, he needed to get the Snowbird through the narrows and in the cove before Dutner caught them. James passed the flashing green light in the narrows a lot closer than he liked and a lot faster than he should have been going, but he could hear the engine of the following boat, speed and slow and speed and slow. Two hard turns and he pushed the Snowbird to 15 knots as she cleared the narrows.

"Lisa take Amy to the bow and hang on tight, the tide is out and I am going to push her right into the sand at the head of the cove. Once she stops you jump and run, right up the trail. Do not look back no matter what you hear do this just like we planned!"

"What about you ..."

"Lisa, do as I say, there's no time he's right behind us."

Lisa grabbed Amy and headed to the bow. James turned the Snowbird into the cove and pushed her to 20 knots and drove her from memory toward the sand and muck at the head of the slight cove. Just as the Snowbirds bow was approaching the muddy beach James pulled the engines to neutral and let her ride her own wake into mud. As the bow grounded the ship was pushed to starboard jerking the ship to a sudden halt. Lisa jumped from the starboard side of the bow into eighteen inches of icy water, lost her balance and fell forward scrapping her knees in the pebbles on the bottom. Once Lisa got herself upright she signaled for Amy to jump and caught her enough to slow her landing in the icy water. Lisa pushed Amy toward the shore told her to move fast and once on the beach they ran into the mist.

As soon as James felt the bow in the muddy sand he killed the engine and the immediately heard how close the following boat was. James went aft out of the wheelhouse and released the stern anchor and let about 35 feet of line out and turned heading back to the bridge.

Two steps toward the bridge and James went down face first onto the deck. At the sound of the shot both Amy and Lisa turned just in time to see James fall, Amy screamed and the twenty-seven-foot boat with Hank in it appeared out of the mist. The scream got Hank's attention away from James and the Snowbird and he looked at the beach. Lisa pushed Amy up the hill and yelled "run up that trail" and they disappeared into the mist and dense forest.

Hank had heard the Snowbird's engine go silent and turned toward where he had heard it last. He slowed the small boat and the stern of the Snowbird appeared and the jerk helping the bitch was there on the stern. He pulled the 45 auto out his jacket and put the engine in neutral at the same time. He aimed at him just as James turned away toward the bridge and squeezed off a round and saw him go down hard. "Got the bastard." Hank exclaimed out loud, then heard the girl scream and saw them on the beach. Hank gunned the engine and drove the small boat right up on the little ramp there at the head of the cove. Once grounded Hank killed the engine without even putting it in neutral and jumped into the icy water from the stern of the boat and headed toward shore, just as he got to the beach he heard a large splash and turned but the mist obscured most of what was behind him in the cove. Hank turned back toward the beach and headed up the trail into the forest.

The 45 slug went through James' left side and sent him to the deck, stunned. James rolled to the right and saw the bullet had gone straight through without hitting any bones or arteries just blasted a big burning hole in muscle. Amy's scream got him to his feet and he went into the bridge and pulled out his keys and opened the narrow locker with the firearms. He grabbed a 44 revolver and a 45 auto both in holsters and stuffed them into a dry bag and dove from the bridge over the starboard side and swam to the cliffs. James swam hard to get around the rock on opposite side of the boat ramp, behind it he knew of a way to climb the cliff to a small ledge that would lead him to the wooded area above the old ruins. Once on the ledge he shuffled along it and pushed through the large black spruce branches that mostly concealed the ledge from the forest. James scrambled up the steep hill climbing several small waist high ledges and then ran through the trees up the hill to the grassy clearing at the top of the plateau. He exited the trees just in time to see Amy and Lisa come over a ridge running on the trail, they saw him and ran to him, both were crying and wanted to hug him but James just grabbed them and started dragging them toward the trees.

"Move into the trees quickly. See where I came up follow it down go now." James pushed Amy into the trees then stopped and handed Lisa the 45 auto. "Follow the blood trail" he pointed the blood trail he had left as he climbed up the hill. "There are three ledges to jump down and a very large spruce tree. The tree hides the ledge push Amy out first and then you go. Wait on the ledge if anyone moves onto that ledge shoot, don't hesitate it won't be me! Got it?"

Lisa did not answer James went down again this round went through his left thigh and he tumbled down into the trees. The sound of the shot made Lisa scream and she headed toward him. "Run, go, go now!" James screamed at her and she ran pushing Amy down the hill in front of her following the trail James has left.

Hank crested the hill and once in the grass saw the bastard and shot him again and came at run marking where the bitch and the girl went into the woods. "Hate the fucking woods" Hank moaned as he slowed, approaching where James had gone down again. Hank moved into the trees where the bitch had run and a large caliber round slammed into the tree inches in front of his face. So close the wood splinters drew blood. Hank dropped as the sound of James' 44 echoed through the grass. "Bastards got a pistol, too bad he's a bad shot." Hank mumbled as he saw James move from behind the large spruce tree and hobble down the slope, stumble, fall and roll off a short ledge of rocks. Hank crawled back up the hill to the grass and then ran along the tree line until he got beyond where James had fallen off the ledge. Hank decided to finish this asshole off then get the bitch and the girl.

James' leg wound was close, but missed bone and arties, lucky again. After sending Lisa down the hill he moved away along the tree line and stopped after twenty yards and stood behind a large spruce and waited until Dutner got level with him and popped off a round at his head hitting the tree just in front of his face. That sent him back and James took off angling away from where he sent Lisa and Amy but still downhill, but he lost his balance and tumble down over the first ledge and lay stunned for a moment. James crawled further along the ledge and the looked up for Dutner and saw him at the edge of the trees moving the same direction as James. James jumped up and hobbled along the ledge as fast as he could through a short opening hoping Dutner would see him and it worked.

Hank saw James move and aimed but James was behind some brush to fast. Then he heard him fall and saw him tumble off the next ledge, from where Hank stood that appeared to be a six to eight foot fall. Hank heard the distinct sound of a man hitting a hard surface with force. Thinking this was his chance he moved quickly down the hill to the first ledge but caught a glimpse of James further along the lower ledge and moving quicker than Hank thought he could. There was quite a bit of blood every place James had stopped and he was leaving a good trail. Hank thought if I push him more he'll bleed out enough to pass out and I can finish this bastard. Hank moved quietly along the upper ridge toward where he had seen James go.

James rolled off the second ledge and hit hard, but was up instantly hobbling as fast as he could along this ledge, it was smoother and more clear than the one above and he knew that in a hundred yards or so the ledges would start to smooth out and turn into thickets of willow and small spruce. After fifty yards or so he stopped to catch his breath, he was losing blood fast by running like this but he couldn't stop now. He looked up and back, Dutner was moving along the upper ridge slowly and cautiously. James wanted to lead him to the willow thicket, so he could get close enough to take him out. James was wishing he was a better shot than he was. He got moving again and hopped and stumbled his way to the willow thicket, then dropped to the ground suddenly.

Hank had seen James stop, then move again, the ledges were smoothing out and he could see more open country ahead, my kind of terrain he thought. Hank followed as James moved again but did not see him drop suddenly just before the willows. Hank moved along the upper ledge until it disappeared. He stopped, looking down at the edge of the thicket he thought he saw the bastard laying there face down. Hank figured loss of blood had caught up with him and started moving toward him gun raised aiming. James heard him moving closer, and lifted his head slightly, the small brown bear was no more than three feet from him, just above he could hear the larger mother bear digging up spring grubs in the willow thicket. Hank was still moving toward him and was so focused on James he did not see either bear. Hank moved to his right closer to the thicket, a place to dive into if the bastard moved to get a shot at him. James grabbed a stick with his left hand and poked the small bear in the ribs which startled it and it bellowed loudly. Hank stopped suddenly and a loud grunt behind him made him turn, the large bear was only a foot behind him.

Hank was bringing the 45 auto up to fire but was way to slow the 800lb mother grizzly ripped his throat out and he went to his knees. Now she towered above him and she dropped on to all four, driving her front paws into his chest. James heard Dutner's ribs break. She then bit hard onto his face and head crushing his skull. James used this moment to go, he got up and moved slowly backward watching her closely as he backed away. The cub had run up the hill above the mother so James was not a threat and was moving away, the bear ignored him and continued ripping at Dutner until he stopped twitching.

James moved backward faster, then turned and moved quickly along the middle ledge. Once out of sight he hobbled as fast as he could back to where he was above the ledge where he had sent Lisa and Amy. "Freddy Mercury" he called out. "Lisa, Amy, its James I need help." James was struggling to stay awake. He sat on the ledge.

It had been a long time since Lisa and Amy had heard gunfire. They heard the sound of the 44 which was different than the sound of the shots that had wounded James. The silence and quiet was more frightening. Amy cried and Lisa tried to keep her quiet but was terrified that James was dead and that Hank was now looking for them. From the vantage point on the ledge they could see the cove and noticed the mist was lifting. Amy watching into the cove said "Mommy a ship."

Lisa looked and saw ship a little larger than the Snowbird appear then saw the stripe on the bow and realized it was a Coast Guard ship and it pulled up to the stern of the Snowbird. "Amy listen that's a helicopter." Lisa exclaimed.

Then Lisa heard the code word and Amy recognized James' voice. Lisa looked out slowly to see James sitting and swaying on the ledge above them. He was soaked in blood and she pulled Amy from the ledge and ran to him. When they got to him Amy started to scream seeing all of the blood, Lisa snapped "shut up and help him." James struggled up the ledge with their help and moved between them. He used Amy as a support on his right and Lisa as a crutch on the left.

"Dutner is dead, he got between a mother grizzly and her cub. Bad move on his part." James explained to them in a gasping voice, "he's back there at the end of the second ledge in the grass just before the willow thicket."

They reached the grassy clearing after a hard struggle and James collapsed just as a Coast Guard helicopter appeared through the breaking mist. James heard it but the sound was far away, he thought he heard voices but they were muffled and distant like a dream. James fell over into the grass and heard and saw no more.

****

James could hear things that made no sense beeps and clicks and voices and movement. What he saw was lights and rooms and things he did not know. He stirred a little then sleep took him again.

James stirred again and opened his eyes, the ceiling was not right, a drop ceiling sound absorbing, grey or dingy white. He lay in a bed with metal sides there were tubes and lines, going into his arm. He remembered what had happened and he turned to the motion he heard next to him.

"Mommy, he's awake." Amy spoke quietly to Lisa who was asleep in a chair. Lisa startled, sat up, looked at James and got up and came to the bed and kissed him.

"How do you feel?" She asked smiling, obviously relieved to see him awake.

"Tired."

"Not surprising with how much blood you lost."

"Where's our boat?"

"The Coast Guard took it to Wrangell yesterday afternoon."

"Yesterday?"

"James it's Monday evening you've been out for over 24 hours."

"Oh crap, I got to get up."

"Oh no you don't you stay put."

"Lisa, I got to pee, let me up so I can use the bathroom."

"Go get the nurse" Lisa told Amy who left the room quickly "you stay still you've been shot, twice."

Just then the nurse came in, "he's awake" he stepped next to the bed opposite Lisa and lowered the rail, "need to use the toilet eh?"

"Yea" James looked at him.

"Okay, let's get you up then." The nurse helped James stand and let him go into the bathroom. James' hospital gown was opened in the back and Amy giggled.

"Mommy, James has a real cute butt."

"Amy" Lisa scolded, "you should not be noticing things like that, but your right he does have a cute butt." Lisa's grin was wide and seeing James stand and walk was heartwarming. She knew he was going to be fine.

Once back in bed James asked Lisa what happened after they got to the grass out of the woods.

"Just as you passed out a Coast Guard helicopter swooped into the clearing and Amy and I waved like crazy and it landed in the center of the grass about 50 yards away. The Coast Guard men came over to help and they brought a stretcher to put you on. Then men from the Coast Guard ship came up and there was a State Trooper with them, I told them where you said Hank was and the Trooper and a couple of the men from the ship went to find his body. You were put on the helicopter, they allowed Amy and I to fly with you to the hospital here in Ketchikan."

"That was so much fun, the helicopter was noisy and bumpy and we could see the ocean and the mountains and glaciers. Was the first time I ever flew, mommy too." Amy pipped in interrupting Lisa's report.

"Yes it was the first time either of us had ever flown, I was too scared you were dying to notice anything." Tears well up in her eyes and she paused to brush them away. "Did you know that you and I have the same blood type?"

James shook his head no, "how would I know that?"

"Well we do. So they took my blood and put it in you. So now you have my blood in you, what do you think of that?"

"I bet that's what saved my life." James grinned his most mischievous grin "thank you for helping me."

"A State Trooper and Coast Guard investigator were here this afternoon they wanted to talk to you, they said they would be back in the morning." Lisa paused "they told me that the Snowbird was taken to Wrangell along with the stolen boat Hank had used."

"I bet they have a lot of questions, but I hope to be out of here before they get here." James shook his head, being questioned was not a favorite of his.

"They also told me that they recovered Hank's body and his gun." Lisa paused, hesitating to tell him that the police took his guns. "I gave them the two guns we had."

Lisa stopped and looked into James' eyes, "you risked your life to save us from him. I am so glad you're okay." She leaned in and kissed him passionately.

"You look like you need to get some sleep. Have you been here since Sunday afternoon?" James looked at her seriously, she nodded. "Did they give you my clothes with keys and wallet and stuff?" Lisa nodded again.

"Well not your clothes, the police took them." James nodded

"You need to take Amy and go to my apartment and get some sleep. There is cash in my wallet get a cab. In the morning you can bring back my laptop and cellular access point, and clean clothes. Tomorrow afternoon we are going to Wrangell by plane to get our ship and get back to work." James smiled at her.

"You're going to get out of the hospital tomorrow? How do you know?" Amy was looking at James like he was crazy.

Lisa put her arm around Amy as Amy looked up "he's going to leave tomorrow no matter what the doctors say." Then looking at James "aren't you?"

"Correct, they cannot force me to stay and I will heal better and faster on the ship, working, than I will here in this crazy place."

"That is absolutely correct. You will heal better and faster away from here." A woman, in her mid-fifties stated bluntly walking into the room. She wore a white coat with a stethoscope in the pocket and her eyeglasses on a lanyard around her neck.

"Doctor Peters, good to see you. How have you been?" James smiled at the her.

"I am fine and you're doing much better I see."

"Doctor this is Lisa my new deck hand and her daughter Amy" James started to introduce them.

"We have met, you need to keep this deck hand James, she is very loyal and dedicated to you has not left since they brought you in."

"I hope to keep her forever" James grinned and then in a serious tone "if she'll have me that is."

"Smart man." Just then a nurse came in with a tray of bandages and other items. "Let's take a look at these wounds and make sure they are clean." Doctor Peters and the nurse checked and redressed the wounds. "You lost a lot of blood so I want to keep you here tonight but tomorrow morning you can go home, or back to your ship." She said bye and they left.

Lisa was still in shock, Amy walked to the other side of the bed and kissed James' cheek, "mommy is speechless James, you surprised her."

"You did" Lisa stammered "did you really mean what you just said?" Lisa paused tears welled up in her eyes "please don't tease me, not about this."

"I did Lisa, I really want you to stay forever, and when we are out of here I will ask formally but not here, not now." James held her hand and smiled.

Tears rolled down her face and they kissed. Soon though James was asleep and Lisa took Amy to their new home in Ketchikan. In the morning their new life together with James would begin.

Made in the USA
Columbia, SC
22 May 2023